# SHIELDS OF OMANAGAR

GAALAV MOHAN
ANKITA PAREEK

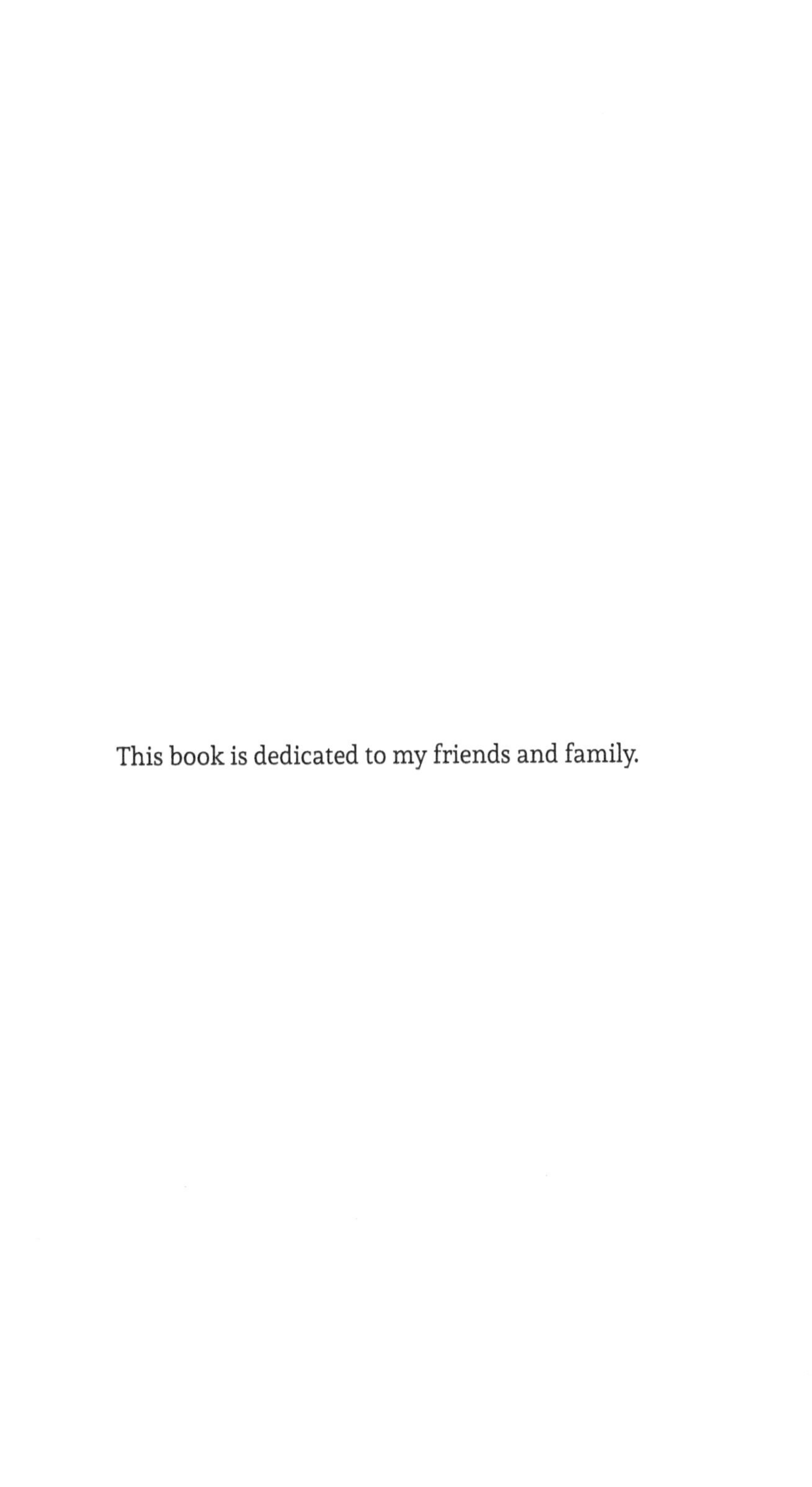

This book is dedicated to my friends and family.

# Contents



**Coming Soon**

# Foreword

"In a world where myth and reality collide, this story unfolds like an ancient prophecy brought to life. What's remarkable about Sheilds of Omnagar VOL. 1 is its ability to seamlessly blend the past and present, inviting the reader into a world filled with mystery, danger, and intrigue. As you read, you'll uncover secrets that feel timeless, yet remain eerily relevant. Gaalav Mohan has created not just a novel, but an experience. Prepare to lose yourself in its pages."

- Rammohan Meena

# Preface

This story began in the quiet hours of the night, when the line between dreams and reality blurs. As I wrote the tale of Ryle, Sarah, and the ancient legend of Omnagar, I was guided by a belief that the past is never truly gone—it lingers, waiting for the right moment to resurface. The idea of the Shields, fractured and hidden, haunted me. And so, I wrote, trying to understand the world I was building—a world that, in many ways, echoes the complexities of our own. This novel is an exploration of memory, betrayal, and power, and I invite you to join me on this journey, as we uncover the secrets buried deep within the story

# ACKNOWLEDGEMENTS

I would like to extend my heartfelt thanks to my editor, Sudha Pareek, whose patience and sharp eye helped refine the world of Omnagar into something I could never have done alone. To my beta reader, Rammohan Meena, thank you for your thoughtful feedback, your enthusiasm, and your belief in this story from the very beginning. To my family, your endless support and understanding while I spent countless hours lost in this world mean more than words can say. And finally, to Ankita Pareek, for encouraging me to keep writing even when the going got tough. Without all of you, this book would not have come to fruition. Thank you for being part of this journey.

# Prologue

Long ago, when the world was young and the legends of Omnagar were only whispers, the Shields were forged in the fire of conflict. Their power was unimaginable, their purpose divine. But like all things born of ambition, they fractured, scattered by those who feared their power. The Master, once a hero, fell from grace. His betrayal split the Kingdom, and the world would never be the same. But in the shadows, the remnants of his legacy linger—waiting. And when the time is right, when the bloodline stirs once again, the Shields will return. And with them, the true test of the world's future will begin.

# I

# The French Stone

There were legends, and myths, and tales without number about Omnagar, that ancient land of mystery and power. Most were frightfully similar, spun from the same age-old thread into variations so small as to be indistinguishable. Yet there was one that stood above all others, a story that had been told time and again, its telling more vivid and compelling each time. This was the tale that found its way into the grand halls and meager hovels of Rostrago, immortalized in vibrant illustrations and fervent retellings, a tale that began with a measure of majesty before descending into terror and woe. It spoke of Omnagar as it was long ago, a wondrous land where life thrived in peace and harmony, a place where the air was filled with the fragrance of blooming hope. But then came a frightful new moon night, and with it a turning of fortune as a sinister figure appeared, a shadow amidst the light. "The Master of the Shields," they called him, an ominous title for the mightiest being in the world unchallenged and alive. What followed were the cruelest of days, days where the sun dared not to rise, and the moon lay hidden behind veils of despair. The Master of the Shields seized Omnagar in his iron grasp, not stopping there but taking Rostrago as well, leaving neither corner nor crevice untouched. He reigned from a place foreboding and cold, Ashencliff, the largest of earthly peaks, a mountain that stabbed at the sky with icy fingers. The Black Legion, his army of darkness, ruthlessly silenced all who dared defy him, their lives extinguished as swiftly as candles doused by a stormy wind. Around him gathered throngs of followers, drawn to him by the shimmering lure of the shields. Each shield, a dazzling prize, controlled the primal forces of earth, and together they promised power rivaling that of the gods. The Master of the Shields was the sole master of them all, unmatched in his terrifying dominion. Yet there was a single force unknown to him, a mystery that eluded even his supreme cunning. This was the French Stone, the one and only thing with the power to strip bare the might of the shields. Forged by the gods themselves, the stone existed expressly to destroy any who wielded the shields with evil in their hearts. The very purpose of the shields was subverted by the Master; they were meant for noble reign, for ruling the earth as a just and good king, not as a tyrant. The outcome was long uncertain, but then came a hero who shifted the balance. Aeirin Thalor, a name sung by the grateful, found the French Stone and struck down the so-called Master, his victory remembered in story and song. The story lingered in the air like smoke, hanging over the assembled with a heaviness that incited both awe and restlessness. "My lord," a rabble of voices broke in from below the dais, desperate and pleading. "What was the Master of the Shields' name?" The crowd surged with the question, pressing toward the King in eagerness and thrill. He paused, savoring the attention, before giving his rueful reply. "Uhmm... only a few know about it," the King said with a mischievous curl to his lips. "And fortunately or unfortunately, I am not one of them." A ripple of curiosity and frustration passed through the gathered listeners as they exchanged glances and mumbled their disbelief. The King allowed the anticipation to build, pacing with deliberate slowness as he measured his next words. "I think," he began with a theatrical flourish, "I think it would be better if you all know about the French Stone." His booming voice cut through the noise like a blade, bringing instant silence. This was what they had come to hear, the core of the legend and the reason for their gathering. "I am sure most of you are aware of it," he continued, pacing with dignified authority. "But for those who don't, I will explain in detail." The King's eyes twinkled with the thrill of storytelling, and he spoke with the fluidity of a bard spinning tales by the fireside. "The Stone, oh yes, the Stone. It is a thing of myth and mystery, a stone made by gods, to make sure that no evil force can rule the earth. No one truly knows where it was made, or how. Such is its mystery, deep and unsolved." The words were like sweet nectar, hypnotizing the ears of the crowd. "The French Stone, you see, it was created to thwart the shields, to defeat them and their master. But, oh, there was a condition to its power. A catch, if you will." He paused dramatically, eyes sweeping the enraptured assembly. "It would only work if the person who found it had no desire to rule. That is why, only good people find it, and evil ones never." A collective murmur rose like the buzzing of a thousand bees, the legend sinking in with its full weight. "Just like Aeirin Thalor," the King pressed on, his voice swelling with conviction. "Just like Aeirin Thalor who found it and defeated the Master of Shields." A tension hung in the silence, as if the crowd itself held its breath, until finally the King spoke again. "People say that when the Master of the Shields was defeated, he lost his mastery of the shields, and his own followers turned against him, killing him the very same night." The story's end brought a gasp of wonder, a tangible excitement that hung stillborn in the chilled air. The King paused, drawing out the moment as he saw the gleaming eyes fixed upon him. "Later," he added, the word a temptation, a promise of more to come, "later it was discovered that the Black Legion were not exactly his supporters at all. Not as we thought." The crowd leaned in, a single body of anticipation. "They were innocents," declared the King, "their bodies and minds bent to the will of the Evil Powers of the shields!" An uproar of shock and amazement rippled through the gathered throng, swirling into a frenzy of disbelief and confusion. "But my lord," cried out a voice that cut above the chaos, "you just said the shields were good. That the shields were made by the gods. How can they have evil powers?" The crowd shifted its gaze back to the King, demanding an answer. With a grandiose wave, he silenced them again, his expression one of serene wisdom. "It depends upon the master," he pronounced with grave certainty, "and his mind." The crowd erupted once more, voices clamoring and competing, some shouting agreement, others dissent, all of them insistent. "How can you say that, my lord?" came the voice of a woman, her tone sharp and inquisitive. "How can you be sure the gods made them? It was thousands of years ago, before any who now live. How can anyone know?" The King smiled with the patience of a sage. "No one really knows who made them," he confessed, "not for sure. It is our belief, my people, just our belief that the gods made them. But believe me," he said, raising his voice to dominate the clamor, "believe me, these are not just stories. That's why you need to know them, and tell them, and learn them. History repeats itself. It is you all who must be ready." The King's words were a rallying cry, a call to arms meant to awaken the spirits of his people. "We never know what comes next," he said with a somber nod. "It is you who will help me defend Rostrago." The people shifted uncomfortably at the sudden urgency in his tone. "Defend our society," he continued passionately. "We must be ready for anything that comes our way." The crowd roared with newfound purpose, some in protest, some in loyalty, some simply in the confusion of the moment. "Thank you for your time," said the King at long last, seeing that he had planted the seed of unrest among them, and he turned back with his two guards, leaving the tumultuous throng behind him.

Whispers and hushed rumors spread like wildfire through the gathered throng, each person struggling to make sense of the King's address. The story, once a distant myth, now felt closer, more real, the threat almost palpable. There was fear in the eyes of the crowd, and uncertainty, and the spark of something dangerous that they could not quite name. They spoke in quick, excited bursts, some insistent on the truth of the tale, others skeptical, all bound together in their eagerness. And then, amidst the chaos, a man in a black robe raised his voice above the din, his hood casting a shadow over his face. "History repeats itself," he said, his words deliberate and ominous. He moved deftly through the crowd, nimble as smoke in a breeze, leaving trails of suspicion in his wake. "But this time it will be different," he whispered to himself, his voice low and resolute. The crowd parted around him, unaware of his purpose but disturbed nonetheless by the conviction in his tone. "This time," he murmured, slipping between clusters of people wrapped in their own shock and uncertainty, "this time it will have to change itself." He wove his way through the milling throng, silent and sure, before disappearing into its depths, leaving nothing but the echo of his words behind him.

"Maybe this time, the story will be different after all." said the hooded man to himself in a deep voice, as he disappeared, leaving everyone whispering and gossiping upon Kings words.

The news reached, the Queen of Rostrago. She was in her palace, talking to a few of her maids. She looked worried and impatient. "Is it true?" she asked. "Yes, Your Highness. King did give a speech and told everything to the people."

"What was the need?" shouted Queen, her voice enough to scare anyone around.

"Ah............"Ryle woke up with a loud scream. He lay panting in his bed, disoriented, the dream still fresh like an echo in his mind. "What happened?" asked his roommate Sarah, glancing up from her desk with a concerned look. "Nothing," replied Ryle, rubbing his eyes and trying to steady his breath. "Nothing, just a wild, strange dream I think." He sat up, his head still swimming with images that seemed at once foreign and familiar. "About what?" Sarah pressed, a curious frown forming on her face. Ryle hesitated, the words hanging in his throat like a mystery waiting to unfold. "I wanted to ask," he began, not sure how to even describe it, "I wanted to ask where Rostrago is?" The name felt heavy on his tongue, like a relic from another time. "Oh come on," Sarah teased, a playful smirk tugging at her lips, "you don't know about Rostrago?" She paused, savoring the moment like a cat with a mouse, then leaned in as though sharing a forbidden secret. She whispered, almost reverently, "The great kingdom of Rostrago." Ryle blinked in bewilderment, the pieces falling together in baffling ways. "Why would I ask you then?" he countered, a mixture of confusion and excitement in his voice. Sarah laughed, the sound light and teasing. "Well," she said, drawing out the word, "Rostrago is no longer a country or a state. It was, but centuries ago." Her words hit him with the force of revelation, the dream now taking on a weighty significance. "My great great great grandfather," Ryle exclaimed suddenly, the realization dawning on him. "I saw the King of Rostrago speaking in my dream. He said his name." Sarah's eyes widened as she made the connection. "You still remember his name?" she asked, her tone half-mocking and half-disbelieving. "Shut up," Ryle retorted, the excitement bubbling beneath his words. "He defeated the Master of the Shields by using the French Stone!" Sarah stared at him, her mouth agape. "Aerin Thalor was your great great great grandfather?" she burst out, her voice tinged with shock and amazement. Ryle nodded, the reality of it all still sinking in. "Yeah," he said, the word almost a breath. "Well, who was the last King of the empire?" he asked, his curiosity insatiable. Sarah's expression grew serious as she searched her memory. "King John 5$^{\text{th}}$," she replied. "It is believed that he was killed by his countrymen after a controversial speech... in the Hall of Betrayal." Ryle repeated the phrase with an incredulous tone, the name sending a chill through him. "Hall of Betrayal!"

"Yeah," Sarah repeated, her voice dropping conspiratorially. "That's what they called it alright. The Hall of Betrayal. Every single person just ganged up on him, left him defenseless. Hard to believe how a story like that just gets lost with time, isn't it?" The weight of her words hung in the air, as Ryle sat frozen, absorbing the link between his dream and Sarah's recounting—a connection that felt at once astonishing, inevitable, and somehow deliberate.

"Or maybe," he speculated, his thoughts unraveling with hesitant clarity, "maybe someone didn't want it to be remembered." It was a chilling suggestion, one that cast the silence around them into something almost tangible—an echo of forgotten history mingling with the uncertainty of the present like a shadow that refused to disappear. "Why would you say that?" Sarah asked, her voice tentative, probing for the truth behind his growing suspicion. Ryle shrugged, caught between doubt and a creeping sense of conviction. "Too strange, isn't it?" he said, the words heavy with implication. "All of this... history that repeats itself?" The question hovered unresolved, an enigma between them that seemed larger than both of their understandings. As if breaking a spell, Sarah decided to change the subject. "Are you sure," she asked, pointing to the jumble of papers scattered across her desk, "are you sure you want to do this?" Ryle blinked, his mind dragging itself back to the present moment with effort. "I'm going to find out more," he declared, an adamant resolve hardening in his voice. He looked at Sarah, his eyes burning with the promise of discovery. "I want to know what happened." Sarah nodded slowly, her expression swinging between support and skepticism like a pendulum. "Okay then," she said, her words trying to be encouraging. "Good luck finding the ghosts of your ancestors." Ryle smirked, the image feeling unexpectedly appropriate. "What are you working on again?" he asked, feigning ignorance to shift the focus from himself. Sarah grinned, the lightness creeping back into her voice. "Just a wild, strange essay," she teased, "on the medieval legends of Europe, your famous forebears included." "About that," Ryle said, his thoughts already drifting back to Rostrago and the tangled web of his lineage. "Do you have any books on it?" Sarah sighed in mock exasperation. "Check the shelves," she said, pointing to the overstuffed bookcase that took up an entire wall of their room, a chaotic monument to her voracious reading habits. "There's bound to be something in that glorious mess." Ryle rose from his bed, a renewed purpose guiding his movements. He scanned the crowded spines, the titles blurring together in a hasty jumble of history and myth, the past calling to him with a siren's song. "Think I'll start with this one," he declared, pulling down a heavy volume whose cover was worn and faded, like a relic from another time. "Good!" Sarah chirped, turning back to her own work with a look of satisfaction. "Maybe you'll find out why they called him the Master of the Shields and not by his actual name." Ryle smirked as he sat back down with the book, flipping through its pages with the air of a man searching for buried treasure. The words leaped out at him, each line pulling him deeper into the same world he had just dreamed—a world that felt both foreign and intimately familiar, as if it were written into his very bones. He read with an intensity that made the hours slip by unnoticed, Sarah's presence all but forgotten as he lost himself in the dense and arcane stories. They mirrored the tales he heard in his sleep, the tale of Rostrago, the King's call to arms, the murmur of dissent, the whiff of betrayal. "Don't read too much or you'll have nightmares again," Sarah said, her teasing voice pulling him back to the real world. He glanced up, shaking his head with a bemused grin, and stretched his legs like a man waking from a deep slumber. "Think I'm going to hit the library," he announced, the decision both impulsive and inevitable, "see if I can track down anything else on this." Sarah watched him, a knowing smile on her face. The sun dipped below the horizon, casting a golden glow over the sprawling campus of Harkstone University. Students lounged lazily on the manicured lawns or hurried to evening classes, backpacks bouncing against their shoulders. Ryle walked briskly across the quad, his mind still spinning with thoughts of Rostrago and the intricate web of legends and history he was only beginning to unravel. The book he had started was gripped tightly in his hand, its cover worn and faded like a relic from another time. The library loomed ahead, a grand stone building that seemed out of place amidst the modern architecture surrounding it.

# II

# The Book That Should Not Exist

The heavy oaken doors of the Harkstone University Library groaned open with a sound that echoed like a distant memory. The scent of parchment and aged wood washed over Ryle as he stepped inside, carrying the book like a talisman in his hand. It felt wrong to be here after hours, but not so wrong. The janitor had left the door ajar. Maybe on purpose. Maybe fate.

A few dim lights glowed along the main reading hall, casting long shadows across shelves that towered like silent sentinels. Ryle moved through the corridors with purpose, his footsteps muffled by the faded red carpet that lined the central aisle.

The library's oldest section—the Special Collections Room—was restricted to students with clearance, but Sarah had once shown him a hidden latch in the nearby Rare Texts chamber. He headed there now, weaving past glass displays of illuminated manuscripts and crumbling atlases.

He reached the back alcove, knelt down, and pressed his fingers to the baseboard Sarah had described. A soft click answered him. A panel swung open, revealing a narrow, spiral staircase of stone leading downward into a space he had never dared to enter alone.

As he descended, the air grew colder, damper. The stone walls closed in, thick with centuries of silence. At the bottom, a narrow corridor opened into a subterranean vault. Dim sconces flickered to life as he stepped forward, reacting to movement—or perhaps, to something else.

The room was small, circular, and lined wall-to-wall with books that looked impossibly ancient. Some were bound in leather faded to ghostly gray, others etched with symbols that defied translation. In the center stood a pedestal.

And on that pedestal sat another book.

Ryle's pulse quickened. It wasn't the book he'd brought with him—this one had found him.

It looked identical to the one he carried—same size, same worn brown leather—but it was colder to the touch, unnaturally so. With trembling hands, he opened it. The pages whispered as they turned, each line written in a spidery hand that danced between languages—some he recognized, some he didn't. But the images were unmistakable.

Omnagar. The Shields. Ashencliff. The Black Legion.

And then—a portrait. Faded, almost erased. A tall, gaunt man in armor black as pitch, his face a blur of menace and shadow.

The Master of the Shields.

Beneath the image, in barely legible script, a name had been etched. But it was scratched out, the ink obliterated.

All but one syllable remained:

"…Varek."

Ryle's breath caught in his throat. Varek. The name thrummed in his ears like a bell tolling from a far-off tower. He didn't know why, but it felt right. As if the name had been waiting for him.

Suddenly, the temperature plummeted. The lights dimmed. And from the shadows behind him, a voice rose—not loud, but unmistakable.

"You shouldn't be here."

Ryle spun, heart hammering. A tall figure stepped into the faint light—cloaked, hooded, the same man from the dream, or… from the crowd. The man who had whispered, "this time, it will have to change itself."

"How did you—?" Ryle began.

The figure raised a hand, silencing him. "You've seen the echoes. You've touched the book. The past is bleeding into you, Ryle Thalor."

Ryle's eyes narrowed. "You know who I am?"

"I know who you were," the man replied, stepping closer. "And what you must become again."

The words struck Ryle like a bolt. His mind reeled.

"This is real?" he asked. "All of it—Rostrago, the Shields, the Stone?"

The man said nothing at first. Then he reached into his cloak and pulled out a shard of pale, crystalline stone, glowing faintly with an inner light.

"The French Stone was never destroyed," the figure said. "It was fractured—scattered to hide it from those who would corrupt it again. One piece lies here. The others… must be found."

Ryle stared, mesmerized.

"Why me?"

"Because," said the man, "you are the last of Aeirin's blood. And the shields stir once more."

A distant bell chimed above them—twelve sharp notes. Midnight.

The man turned toward the corridor.

"There are others searching, Ryle. People who remember more than they should. People who would wake the Master."

"And you?" Ryle called after him. "Who are you?"

The figure paused in the doorway, only his voice remaining behind.

"I am no one," he said. "But I was once called Vaelen."

And then he was gone.

Ryle stood in the silence, the cold stone in his palm pulsing with quiet, terrifying promise.

The moment the hooded man—Vaelen—vanished into the shadows, Ryle felt the air shift again, thickening like mist around his body. He glanced down at the shard of the French Stone in his palm. It glowed faintly, cold but not unpleasant—its pulse syncing with his own heartbeat. The sensation was surreal, yet deeply grounding.

His breath came in slow, deliberate pulls as he tried to steady the storm raging inside him.

He stared at the doorway where Vaelen had stood, then turned back to the pedestal. The second book—the one that mirrored the volume he'd brought from Sarah's collection—was still open, its pages fluttering despite the still air.

Drawn to it again, he flipped through the brittle parchment until something caught his eye.

A map.

Old, hand-drawn, and stained with age. But the places... they were the same as his dream. Rostrago, in bold letters.

Ashencliff, drawn as a towering spear of black rock, surrounded by symbols. Omnagar in the lower east, marked by a sunburst crest. The sea to the west was named The Mourning Deep, and above all that, sprawled across the page in winding runes, were the words:

"He Who Holds the Shields Holds the World."

Ryle's hand traced the map as if it were sacred. The parchment was rough beneath his fingertips. And as he studied it, he noticed something strange—pinpricks of light glowing at certain locations. Four in total.

One of them was blinking softly—here, right below the library.

He looked around slowly, the realization settling like lead in his chest.

This whole university... it was built on something. Something ancient.

There was no time to think it through.

The French Stone shard in his hand suddenly flared with heat—not burning, but urgent. A hum buzzed in his bones. The book's pages flipped on their own, rapidly, until they landed on a section titled:

"Of the Broken Shields and the Curse of Varek."

Ryle read, the words branding themselves into his mind:

When the Master fell, the shields did not die. Scattered, sealed, some destroyed—but most endured. Their hunger remained. Without a true bearer, they poison the mind. They whisper, call, and lure those with fractured souls.

The Master was not born evil. He was made so—by pride, by pain, by betrayal.

And he was not alone.

Ryle froze. The legend had always focused on one man—the tyrant, the conqueror. But this passage implied more. Others.

Before he could dwell on it, the ground beneath his feet gave a subtle tremor. Dust shook loose from the ceiling. A low, echoing rumble reverberated from beyond the stone wall behind the pedestal.

Then came the voice again.

But not Vaelen's.

No. This was different. Ancient. Twisting. Malevolent.

"The blood has awakened… and the seal is weakening…"

Ryle stumbled back. The book slammed shut with a thunderous clap, knocking him off balance. He caught himself on the edge of the pedestal, heart pounding in his ears. The shard of the French Stone in his hand went dark.

The whisper came again, this time clearer.

"You are his blood… and blood remembers…"

Ryle scrambled up the steps, taking two at a time, the musty corridor pressing in around him. As he reached the secret latch and burst into the Rare Texts room, he slammed the hidden panel shut behind him.

Silence returned, but it was an uneasy silence. A silence that knew.

He emerged into the main hall, breathing heavily, as if he'd surfaced from a nightmare. The library's usual warmth felt foreign now, like a mask that no longer fit. He turned sharply when he heard a footstep.

"Ryle?"

Sarah's voice cut through the dark.

She stood near the entrance, wrapped in her hoodie, holding a flashlight. Her brow was furrowed with worry. "What are you doing here?"

"I—" He faltered. "How did you find me?"

"You weren't answering your phone. And you took that book. I figured you'd come here." She took a few steps forward. "You okay? You look like you've seen a ghost."

"I think I did," he muttered, and sank into a nearby bench.

Sarah sat next to him, her eyes sharp with concern. "What happened?"

Ryle handed her the shard of the French Stone. She stared at it, confused, then touched it—and immediately yanked her hand back.

"Cold," she whispered. "And... weird."

"It's part of the French Stone," he said. "The real one. One of its pieces, at least."

She didn't laugh. That surprised him.

"You're serious," she said quietly. "What did you see?"

"I found a hidden chamber," Ryle began. He recounted the pedestal, the second book, the map, the voice—everything. He left nothing out, not even the part about Varek. Sarah listened with the intensity of someone who wanted to believe but didn't know how.

When he finished, she just sat there for a moment.

"That name," she said finally. "Varek."

"What about it?"

"I've seen it before. Somewhere in the archives. I thought it was just a fragment, an old translation error. It was marked next to a name that had been redacted from the original texts. One that was connected to..." Her voice trailed off.

"To what?"

"To the original betrayal."

Ryle's stomach tightened. "You mean the Hall of Betrayal? The one where King John V was killed?"

Sarah nodded. "What if that wasn't the end of the kingdom? What if it was just... the second act?"

They sat in silence.

Then Sarah stood abruptly.

"We need to go back," she said.

"What?"

"To the hidden room. Show me the book."

Ryle hesitated. "It's dangerous."

"Since when did that stop us?"

Ryle cracked a grin despite the gnawing dread inside. "You're insane."

"No," Sarah said, marching toward the darkened stairwell. "I'm curious. And you clearly need someone to keep you alive."

Ryle followed. He didn't know what they were stepping into—but he knew one thing:

The story wasn't finished.

Not yet.

# III

# The Seal Beneath

The air felt heavier the second time Ryle descended the spiral stairs.

This time, he wasn't alone.

Sarah followed close behind, her flashlight beam dancing along the stone walls. The silence between them wasn't awkward—it was dense with questions neither of them had the courage to voice just yet.

When they reached the bottom, the sconces again lit themselves, flaring to life like watchful eyes.

Sarah let out a low whistle. "Okay... I officially take back everything I said about your imagination."

Ryle didn't smile. His eyes were fixed on the pedestal in the center. The book still sat there—closed, but humming with presence, like a coiled spring.

He held out the shard of the French Stone.

It remained dark in his palm, but Sarah stepped back anyway. "Still cold," she muttered.

Ryle moved to the pedestal. "The book flipped on its own before. Showed me things."

"Well, maybe this time it'll give us some answers."

He hesitated, then opened the cover. The pages didn't flutter as before—they waited.

Sarah joined him, peering over his shoulder. "What are we looking for?"

He didn't answer. He didn't know.

Then a pulse ran through the chamber. A subtle tremor beneath their feet. The lights dimmed slightly, and the stone wall behind the pedestal—where the rumble had come from earlier—shimmered faintly. Ryle turned toward it.

"There's something behind that," he said.

Sarah moved to inspect it, running her hands along the worn stone. "Looks solid."

Ryle reached into his pocket and pulled out the shard. The moment it neared the wall, lines of runes lit up across the stone's surface—like frost racing across glass.

Sarah jumped back. "Okay, what did you do?"

"I think it's reacting to the shard."

The runes glowed brighter, and then the stone groaned. A seam split down the center, and with a grinding noise that echoed like ancient thunder, the wall began to open inward—revealing a hidden chamber beyond.

They stepped through.

The room inside was vast—far larger than it should have been beneath the library. Its ceiling arched impossibly high, supported by black marble columns etched with symbols that shimmered like starlight. At the far end, on a raised platform, stood six pedestals in a circle, each empty. And in the center—another pedestal, cracked down the middle.

"The Seal," Ryle murmured.

Sarah stared at the circle. "This feels... wrong."

A whisper stirred the air—faint, unintelligible, like voices trapped in another time. Ryle stepped forward, drawn to the central pedestal. The shard in his hand glowed again, and the whispers stopped.

A single word echoed in his mind:

"Awakened."

He recoiled slightly.

Sarah noticed. "What did you hear?"

"Not hear. Feel." He hesitated, then stepped onto the platform. As he did, one of the six outer pedestals lit up with a soft blue glow.

Sarah blinked. "Did you do that?"

"I didn't touch it."

The glow pulsed once... and then vanished.

"Six pedestals," Sarah said slowly. "Six Shields?"

Ryle nodded. "And one in the center. The Master's?"

Before either could say more, the ground shuddered violently beneath them. Dust fell from the ceiling. From the cracks in the central pedestal, black mist began to seep upward, slow and snakelike.

Sarah backed away. "I really don't like this."

Neither did Ryle. The mist writhed, reaching toward him, and the shard in his hand flared bright, forcing the black tendrils to retreat with a hiss.

Then, from high above in the arched chamber, a voice rang out—calm, sharp, and unmistakably human.

"Step away from the Seal."

Ryle and Sarah turned in unison. A figure stood on the balcony overhead, silhouetted against the glow of unseen sconces. Cloaked in gray, but not hiding.

A woman's voice.

"You don't know what you're playing with," she continued, descending a set of stairs that had materialized from the wall.

Sarah stood protectively in front of Ryle. "Who are you?"

The woman stopped at the base of the steps. Her eyes glinted like iron beneath her hood.

"I'm a Keeper," she said. "And that—" she pointed to the shard in Ryle's hand—"should have stayed buried."

Ryle tightened his grip. "You know what this is?"

"I know what it can become if you keep waking things best left forgotten."

"Vaelen said—"

"Vaelen is a fool," she snapped. "A ghost clinging to guilt."

Sarah stepped forward. "Then help us understand. We didn't come here to break anything."

The woman's eyes flicked to Sarah, then back to Ryle. "You've already broken the Seal's dormancy. It's no longer asleep. And now that it's stirring... others will come."

"Others?" Ryle asked.

"Seekers. Remnants. Shadows. Those who remember what it was like when Varek ruled." Her voice dropped. "Not all wish to keep the past buried."

Ryle looked back toward the pedestal. The black mist had disappeared—for now.

"We need to find the other pieces of the French Stone," he said. "To stop this."

The woman studied him for a long moment. "You sound like him."

"Who?"

"Aeirin."

Silence fell.

Then she sighed. "If you're truly his blood, you'll need more than good intentions. The first piece is yours. But the others are not unguarded."

"Where are they?" Sarah asked.

The woman looked between them.

"Ashencliff. And the lost spire of Caldrin's Hollow."

Ryle's breath caught. He remembered those names from the map.

She turned toward the stairs again. "You'll need a guide. And a blade."

"Wait—what's your name?" Ryle called after her.

She paused.

"My name," she said, "was once Leira. But now I serve the Silent Circle."

And then she vanished into the dark.

Ryle and Sarah stood alone once more in the vast, echoing chamber.

The glow from the central pedestal flickered again—stronger now. Hungrier.

Sarah touched his shoulder. "We're not going back to class anytime soon, are we?"

Ryle shook his head. "No. This is bigger than us."

She looked at the six pedestals. "Then I guess it's time to find the others."

And with the shard pulsing like a heartbeat in his hand, Ryle knew:

The quest had begun.

Absolutely! Here's an extended and deeper continuation of Chapter 3: The Seal Beneath, picking up directly from where the last section left off. This portion expands on the atmosphere, gives more emotional depth to Sarah and Ryle's reactions, hints at an ancient connection between Ryle and the other Shields, and introduces the first ripple of outside danger—setting up future conflict.

The chamber felt colder after Leira vanished.

Ryle stared into the shadows where she had stood, her last words echoing like a drumbeat in his skull: The Silent Circle... Ashencliff... Caldrin's Hollow...

Names from a world that shouldn't exist—and yet somehow did. His fingers curled around the shard, its cold light still flickering faintly. The stone pulsed in rhythm with his breath now. Or maybe it was his breath that had started matching it.

Sarah stepped to the nearest of the six outer pedestals. The surface was blank stone, but the base bore inscriptions—runes curling like vines. "They feel old," she murmured. "Older than writing. Like the language is trying to remember itself."

Ryle moved beside her. "You ever seen anything like this in the archive?"

She shook her head. "Not even close."

As he reached out to touch the rune, the surface shimmered—and an image flickered to life in the air above it. A shield. Simple in shape but marked by a curling serpent etched down its center. The metal looked burned, almost charred, and it hovered there like a memory too stubborn to die.

Then came a sound—distant, echoing—a clang of steel on stone.

Sarah turned sharply. "Did you hear that?"

"I did." Ryle scanned the chamber. The noise had come from beyond the far columns—deep in the shadows at the back of the vault, where the sconces didn't reach.

"Something's back there," he said.

"Something," Sarah echoed.

They didn't have to wait long to find out.

A second clang rang out, louder this time—closer. Then a low, scraping hiss, like rusted armor dragging across stone. Ryle backed toward the main pedestal, holding up the shard like a weapon, though he wasn't sure what it could do.

And then they saw it.

A figure emerged from the dark—not fully human, not fully whole. Its armor was ancient, rusted, fused to its skin. One arm hung limp, the other clutched a jagged blade pitted with rot. Its face was a void of shadow beneath a half-shattered helm.

A wraith—but not a ghost.

It moved like something bound by duty, not death.

Sarah grabbed his arm. "What is that?"

"I don't know. But I think it's guarding the Seal."

The wraith turned toward the central pedestal. As the shard glowed brighter in Ryle's hand, it gave a distorted hiss—almost a word.

"Thalor…"

Ryle's blood froze.

"It knows me," he whispered.

The creature raised its sword and began to advance.

Instinct kicked in. Ryle stepped between Sarah and the wraith, holding the shard high. "Stay back!"

The shard's glow intensified—blinding for a heartbeat—and a ripple of force erupted outward. The wraith was thrown back, slamming against a marble column. Its body cracked like brittle wood. Then it dissolved into smoke, the blade clattering to the stone floor with a dull ring.

Silence fell again. The glow from the shard dimmed.

Sarah let out a breath she'd been holding. "Did you just destroy that thing?"

"I don't know. I didn't mean to." He turned the shard over in his hand. It was quiet again. Still.

Sarah approached the fallen blade cautiously. "It left this behind." She knelt, picked it up with a cloth from her satchel. "It's heavier than it looks."

Ryle looked around. "There might be more."

"I think that was a warning," she said.

He nodded. "Someone—or something—is trying to keep us away from the Seal."

Sarah eyed the center of the platform. "Or from activating it."

As they walked back to the pedestal, Ryle glanced at the surrounding symbols. He could almost hear them—faint whispers pulling at the edges of his thoughts.

"You are his blood... and blood remembers..."

"What if the pedestals are keys?" Sarah said suddenly.

Ryle looked at her. "Keys to what?"

She pointed to the center, where the largest pedestal remained cracked but untouched by light. "If each of the six shields represents a bearer—maybe they each have to be found, reawakened. Only then does the center reveal itself."

"Like restoring the circle," Ryle said.

"Or binding it again."

A shiver ran through him. "Vaelen said the shields stir without bearers. They corrupt."

Sarah looked up at the glowing runes. "So if we don't find the other pieces... others might."

They stood in silence.

Then Ryle spoke. "I need to see Ashencliff."

Sarah nodded slowly. "I'll help you."

He glanced at her. "You don't have to."

She smiled faintly. "You'd die without me."

He chuckled despite the dread curling in his stomach. "Probably."

Sarah stepped closer. "Before we go... there's something I didn't tell you."

Ryle's smile faded. "What is it?"

She took a breath. "My mother—before she died—she used to talk about a 'circle of guardians.' She said they protected something buried beneath the old kingdoms. Something that could reshape the world. I thought she was just... gone. Sick."

"But she wasn't," Ryle whispered.

"No." Sarah looked around the chamber. "She knew."

He placed a hand on her shoulder. "We'll figure it out. Together."

She nodded once. "Then let's start with the archives. If Caldrin's Hollow is real, it has to be somewhere in the records."

"And Ashencliff?"

"West of the old riverline. Near the borderlands. But if it's like it was on that map... it won't be easy to reach."

Ryle turned to the steps. "Then we better start soon. Before someone else gets there first."

As they left the chamber, the sconces dimmed again—responding to their departure. The stone wall sealed behind them, closing with a final hiss.

But deep below, something remained awake.

The six pedestals pulsed faintly, like breaths drawn in slumber.

And in the far shadows—unseen—another figure watched from beyond the columns. Its form blurred and shifting, its eyes burning like coals.

It did not speak.

It did not need to.

For it had waited long enough.

# IV

# Ashencliff

The wind howled through the jagged cliffs of Ashencliff, the sound of it crashing against the ancient stones as if the very mountain was alive and in pain. Waves pounded the shores below, foaming violently against the black rocks that stood like teeth jutting from the sea, relentless and unforgiving. Above, the storm clouds churned in a swirl of gray and dark, their edges tinged with an unnatural red glow. The sky was an unbroken expanse of turmoil, and within it, Ashencliff stood, an ancient fortress carved from the heart of the mountain itself. The place felt as if it had always been here, its walls soaked in the history of battles fought long before the world had changed. But Ashencliff was not merely a relic. It was a place of power—a place where things darker than history were made to come alive again.

Inside the fortress, the stone walls felt as though they were breathing—slow, heavy breaths that echoed in the chambers. Torches flickered along the long, narrow corridors, casting wild, dancing shadows across the blackened stone. The air was thick with the scent of iron and oil, the musk of leather, and something more—the smell of ancient rituals.

At the heart of this stone labyrinth stood Verya, her silhouette dark and imposing against the flickering torchlight. She stood alone in the command hall, her back straight, her gaze fixed on the map that stretched out before her. The Black Legion had been growing steadily, and tonight they would make their move. She had already made her decisions, and all that remained was the execution. The map detailed the locations of the French Stone shards—fragments scattered across the world, hidden away, waiting to be rediscovered. Verya had been preparing for this moment for years, learning every myth, every secret, and now, the time had come to claim what was hers.

Her heart pulsed with cold resolve as her fingers traced the edges of the map. The French Stone would be the key to unlocking the ancient power of the Shields. She had studied it all—watched the slow unraveling of history through forgotten texts and the whispers of the dead.

She had once been a scholar—a seeker of knowledge, her mind consumed by the pursuit of understanding things that others could not even fathom. She had spent years traveling through ruined cities, deciphering texts older than the kingdoms that had come and gone. But in the end, her search had led her to this place: the Black Legion.

Verya had not joined the Legion out of a thirst for war or conquest. She had not been seduced by the idea of power, as most might have been. No, her motivations were different. Her obsession with the Shields, with the fractured French Stone, and with the legends that whispered of a power beyond understanding had driven her here. She had discovered the truths buried beneath the surface of the world—truths that only the Black Legion had the strength to uncover.

And so, she had taken the mantle of leader, her cold intellect and unwavering will guiding the Legion to new heights. Under her command, the Legion was no longer just a mercenary group; they were something darker, more dangerous, and more devoted to their cause than ever before. They were fanatical, bound by loyalty to a single idea, a single truth: the return of the Master, and the power of the Shields.

Verya's thoughts were interrupted by the sound of footsteps behind her, the echo of armored boots clanging softly against the stone floor. She turned, her face as unreadable as ever, to see one of her most trusted officers enter. His expression was tense, his posture rigid.

"Commander," he began, his voice low and respectful. "The scouts have returned."

Verya raised an eyebrow, her lips curling into a faint, almost imperceptible smile. "And?" she asked, her voice like ice.

"They've found something," the officer continued. "A fragment. It's hidden in the mountains near the temple of Omnagar. It's well-guarded, but we can take it."

"Good," she replied flatly. "Prepare the Legion. We leave at dawn."

The officer hesitated for a moment before nodding. "Yes, Commander."

As he turned to leave, Verya's mind raced. The pieces of the French Stone were scattered across the world, hidden from view, buried beneath centuries of earth and time. But they were never truly lost. Not for someone like her. She had studied the old texts, the forbidden ones—the ones that spoke of the Shields and the Master, of the bloodlines that had been torn apart in an age long gone. She had uncovered the locations, the clues that others had missed, and now it was all coming together. Piece by piece, the world would fall back into its rightful order. But first, she needed the Stone. She needed its power.

She moved towards the large table in the center of the room, where a tome lay open. Its pages were worn, faded, but its contents were clear to her mind. It was the book that had started it all—an ancient manuscript she had found years ago, buried deep within the archives of a forgotten library. The text was old, written in a language few could read, but it held the key to everything she sought.

Her fingers traced the inked lines of the pages, absorbing the words like a thirsting soul. The book spoke of the French Stone, of the Shields that had once ruled the world, and of the Master—Varek. The name haunted her, a shadow that loomed over her thoughts. She knew the stories—knew the myths—but she had come to understand that myths were often born from truths too dangerous to be told.

The Master had been a man of immense power, a ruler who had once held the world in his grasp. But his greed, his hunger for more, had brought about his fall. The Shields had been scattered, hidden away, and the world had been left to pick up the pieces. But the Shields did not die. They endured, waiting for the right hands to claim them once again.

Verya's lips curled into a small smile as she closed the book with a snap. The time was almost here. The fragments of the Stone were coming together, and with them, the power of the Shields would return. She would be the one to claim that power, and with it, the Legion would become unstoppable.

She moved toward the window, her sharp gaze scanning the horizon where the storm was growing fiercer. The sea below foamed angrily, as if protesting the fate that was soon to befall the world. But Verya was unmoved. The storm was merely the beginning.

The Black Legion would march tomorrow. They would take the fragment near Omnagar, and soon after, they would find the others. Ryle Thalor might be out there, somewhere, searching for his own answers—but he would not stand in her way. She had studied him, learned about his bloodline, his connection to the Shields. He was nothing more than an obstacle to be removed, a pawn in a game far larger than he could ever understand.

But there was something else, something nagging at her. The name Varek—she had heard it before, whispered among the oldest texts, the oldest prophecies. Was he truly gone? Or had he merely been waiting, biding his time for the right moment to return?

Verya stood there for a long moment, staring out into the storm. The Black Legion was waiting for her. The storm was waiting for her. And the world itself was on the cusp of change. She would lead them all into a new age, an age where the power of the Shields would rise again, and where she—no one else—would be the one to wield it.

Tomorrow, they would move.

But tonight... tonight, the darkness of Ashencliff wrapped around her like an old, familiar cloak.

# V

# The Echoes of
Ashencliff

The wind howled through the jagged cliffs of Ashencliff, carrying with it the scent of salt and decay. The black stone walls of the fortress seemed to exhale their own darkness as they loomed above the churning sea below. Ashencliff had always been a place of menace—its history buried in blood and betrayal, its future uncertain, but under Verya's leadership, it had become something more: a stronghold of power, a crucible where the Black Legion would forge its future.

Verya stood at the high balcony of the fortress, looking out over the stormy ocean, her eyes cold and unblinking. The wind whipped her black cloak around her body, but she remained unmoved, her hands clasped tightly behind her back. Her face was as pale as the moonlight that filtered through the dark clouds above. The weight of her responsibilities was not lost on her. The Black Legion was not just a faction—it was an idea, a movement, an answer to the ancient struggles that had never truly ended.

Below her, in the heart of Ashencliff, the Legion's soldiers moved like shadows in the courtyard, training, preparing, ever watchful. The Black Legion had grown in strength under her command, but its true power lay not in numbers, but in the unwavering loyalty of those who followed her. They believed in the cause—whatever that cause might truly be. For Verya, it was simple. Power. Control. Revenge. All in service of a fractured world that had long since abandoned its idealism.

Her thoughts were interrupted by the heavy footsteps of a messenger, his boots echoing off the stone floor as he approached.

"Lady Verya," he called respectfully, bowing slightly as he came to a stop. "Word from the scouts. The search for the shards of the French Stone continues. They've uncovered a lead in a village near the coast. It's... possible that another piece lies there."

Verya's eyes narrowed. She had known this day would come. The search for the French Stone had been relentless. The fragments of the shattered relic had been scattered for centuries, hidden from those who would abuse them, but she knew the truth. The French Stone was not just a piece of history—it was the key to something far greater. The Black Legion had only one purpose now: to gather the shards before anyone else could.

"Prepare the troops," Verya ordered, her voice low but unmistakably commanding. "We leave at dawn. No one must know of our movements."

The messenger nodded quickly and turned to depart, but before he could go, Verya called after him.

"And bring me the map. The one from the archives," she added, her tone colder than the sea winds. "I want to see where the other pieces are. It's time we took what is ours."

The man hesitated, then nodded again and left, disappearing into the depths of the fortress. Verya remained standing by the balcony, her thoughts turning inward. The past was an echo she could never silence, a wound that had never healed. Her life, once devoted to knowledge and understanding, had been shattered by betrayal. The Black Legion had offered her a path forward—one filled with darkness, yes, but also with the potential for power. The kind of power that could bend the world to her will.

A power that could rewrite the past.

She had been a scholar once, before everything changed. A researcher at the Royal Academy of Lyse in the far reaches of the kingdom, where she had delved into ancient texts and forgotten lore. It was there that she had first learned of the Shields—the ancient order that had once protected the kingdom. She had studied the old tomes, deciphering cryptic prophecies and forgotten names, driven by a thirst for knowledge that consumed her.

But it was also there that she had uncovered the truth about the betrayal that had torn the kingdom apart—King John V's death at the hands of his own council. The broken legacy of Rostrago, the kingdom that had once ruled with iron and fire. It was a truth she could not ignore.

But as she dug deeper, her passion for discovery had turned into an obsession. The more she uncovered, the more she realized that the truth was far darker than she could have imagined. And in that moment, she had made a choice—a choice to join the Black Legion. To embrace the darkness that had always been there, lurking beneath the surface of the world.

Now, as the leader of the Legion, she could feel the weight of that choice pressing down on her. But she also felt something else—a stirring within her, a sense that the pieces of a grand puzzle were falling into place. The French Stone, the fractured Shields, the ancient power that had once been wielded by the Kings of Rostrago—it was all connected. And Verya would be the one to harness it.

"Lady Verya," a voice broke through her thoughts. She turned to see a tall figure standing in the doorway, his posture rigid. He was one of her most trusted lieutenants, a warrior named Kaelen. His armor gleamed in the dim light, and his expression was as cold and calculating as her own.

"The scouts have returned," Kaelen reported. "They've found the village. It's isolated, but there's word of a stranger—a traveler who has been asking questions. Someone is getting too close."

Verya's eyes flashed with interest. "A traveler? A spy, perhaps?"

"We're not sure," Kaelen replied, his tone serious. "But we believe he's connected to someone important. The villagers are nervous. They don't trust him."

Verya's gaze hardened. She had no patience for complications, no tolerance for the weak-minded. The Black Legion was built on strength, and those who failed to see that would be discarded.

"Do we know who he is?" she asked, her voice like steel.

Kaelen hesitated. "We believe it's someone named Ryle Thalor. He's been asking about the Shields."

At the mention of the name, Verya's eyes narrowed further. Ryle Thalor. The name sounded familiar, but she could not place it.

"Thalor..." she muttered, her mind racing. "Do we know where he is now?"

"We believe he's in the village, yes. If you wish, I can take a team and deal with him before he becomes a problem."

Verya's lips curled into a faint smile, a predator's smile.

"No," she said, her voice calm but dangerous. "I will deal with this myself. Prepare the Legion. We move out at dawn."

Kaelen nodded, his expression unreadable. He turned and left without another word, disappearing into the shadows of the fortress. Verya stood there for a moment longer, gazing out over the sea, her thoughts churning.

Ryle Thalor. The name felt like a puzzle piece that didn't quite fit. She had heard whispers of someone with that name—someone connected to the ancient power of the Shields. But how could that be? She had been the one to uncover the truth, to piece together the scattered remnants of the past. If this Ryle Thalor was involved in this ancient drama, he would not stand in her way.

She would make sure of that.

As the night deepened, she retreated into the shadows of Ashencliff, preparing herself for the next step in this dangerous game. The future of the Black Legion—and of the world—hung in the balance. And she would be the one to seize it.

The pieces were coming together. The French Stone would be hers. And when it was, no one would be able to stand against her.

Verya had always believed that the end justified the means. But now, she could see the path to power more clearly than ever before. The Black Legion would rise. Ashencliff would become the center of a new empire—a kingdom ruled not by the weak, but by those with the strength to claim what was rightfully theirs.

And in the end, she would be the one to wield the Shields.

No one could stop her now.

The next morning, the mist over Ashencliff was thick, rolling in from the sea like a veil of secrecy, wrapping the fortress in its cold embrace. The Black Legion stirred in the pre-dawn hours, their movements disciplined and deliberate. Each soldier knew their place, their purpose, their duty. They had been forged in the fires of battle, tempered by the harsh winds of loyalty, and under Verya's command, they were an unstoppable force.

In the war room, dimly lit by torches that flickered like dying embers, Verya stood before a large map of the region, her fingers tracing the lines of the coastline. Her thoughts were sharp and focused, like the blade of a dagger. The village where the scout had found the potential shard of the French Stone was a small, inconsequential place in the grand scheme of things, yet it had become the center of her world. A world she was determined to reshape in her image.

The map was littered with marks—locations of known fragments of the French Stone, places where the Shields had been rumored to lie hidden, and villages where whispers of ancient power had surfaced. Verya had always prided herself on her strategic mind, her ability to see the threads connecting events, people, and places. She had learned long ago that control wasn't just about power—it was about knowledge. Knowledge of the world. Knowledge of your enemies. And above all, knowledge of yourself.

Her hand hovered over a particular mark on the map, a small, nameless village nestled on the outskirts of the kingdom. It was there that the piece of the French Stone had been discovered. But it was also there that Ryle Thalor had surfaced. His name had been whispered by the scouts, and though she had not yet made the connection, something about him unsettled her. There was an air of familiarity about him, something she could not quite place. She had never been one to let things go unexplained.

"Lady Verya," Kaelen's voice broke through her thoughts, cold and composed as always. He stood in the doorway, his silhouette framed by the flickering light from the torches. His presence was commanding, yet his eyes betrayed nothing.

"Has the Legion been prepared?" Verya asked, not looking up from the map. Her fingers twitched, a subtle movement, like a serpent preparing to strike.

"Yes," Kaelen replied. "We are ready to move. The troops are assembling in the courtyard."

"Good," she said, finally turning to face him. Her expression remained impassive, a mask of cold determination. "This mission must be swift. We cannot afford any delays. If Ryle Thalor is in that village, we need to find him—before he finds what we are looking for."

Kaelen nodded and stepped forward, placing a sealed scroll on the table before her. It was the same one he had mentioned earlier—the one containing the map from the archives, the one that detailed the potential locations of the remaining shards. Verya took the scroll and unrolled it carefully, her eyes scanning the intricate drawings and faded runes that adorned the page.

The map was old, far older than anything she had encountered in the archives of Ashencliff. The markings on the map seemed to pulse with an ancient energy, as though the very parchment was alive with the memory of forgotten kings and battles long past. One symbol, in particular, caught her eye: a circle, surrounded by runes, etched with a symbol she recognized—one she had seen only once before in the royal archives. It was the mark of the Shields.

"This," she murmured, her fingers tracing the circle on the map. "This is the center of it all. The heart of the Shields' power. If this is where the final shard lies..."

She didn't finish the thought. Kaelen was already well aware of the significance. The final shard. The one that would complete the French Stone. The one that would allow her to seize control of the ancient power that had once shaped the kingdom.

"The Legion will not fail," Kaelen said, his voice steady. "We will find the piece before anyone else does."

Verya's lips curled into a smile, but it was devoid of warmth. "They will try," she said softly, more to herself than to Kaelen. "But they won't succeed."

She rolled the map back up and handed it to him. "Gather the troops. We leave at once."

As the Legion prepared to march, Verya stood at the edge of the courtyard, watching them with an air of detached calculation. Her soldiers were ready. There was no doubt in her mind about their loyalty or their ability to follow orders. She had built the Black Legion from the ground up, using her knowledge of the kingdom's fractured history and her ruthless understanding of power. Now, it was time to see her vision realized.

The soldiers donned their black armor, their faces hidden beneath darkened helms. The sound of hooves echoed through the courtyard as riders mounted their steeds, ready to transport the Legion to the village. The storm clouds above seemed to deepen as the wind picked up, carrying with it the scent of rain and salt.

Verya mounted her own horse, the reins tight in her gloved hands. The moment she had been waiting for was approaching. The Black Legion would find the final piece of the French Stone, and with it, they would unlock the power that had been buried for centuries. The echoes of the past were calling her, and she was ready to answer.

The journey to the village was uneventful at first, the sounds of the soldiers' hooves filling the silence as they rode through the dense forest surrounding Ashencliff. The fog grew thicker the further they traveled, swirling around them like a living thing, as though the very earth itself was shrouded in mystery.

As they neared the village, Verya could feel the tension in the air. Something was not right. The stillness of the forest seemed unnatural, as though it was holding its breath in anticipation. The scouts had reported that the villagers were nervous, but there was more to it than that. There was fear.

Verya signaled for the Legion to halt as they reached the outskirts of the village. She could see the thatched roofs of the small cottages, the smoke rising from chimneys, and the faint glow of lanterns through the mist. But something was off. The streets were eerily quiet, and the villagers seemed to be hiding in their homes, watching from behind shuttered windows.

"Stay alert," Verya commanded, her voice low but carrying through the ranks. "We are looking for one man, and one man only. Ryle Thalor. If he is here, he will know we are coming."

Kaelen dismounted and approached her, his eyes scanning the village with military precision. "Shall we begin the search?" he asked.

Verya nodded. "We'll start with the inn. If he's hiding in plain sight, that's where he'll be."

As they moved toward the center of the village, the tension in the air thickened. The villagers watched them from the shadows, their eyes wide with fear, but no one dared to speak. Verya's gaze swept over them, noting their silence, their reluctance to make eye contact. She could sense the unease rippling through the village, a gnawing feeling that this was not just a simple search for a fugitive.

She reached the inn at the heart of the village, its windows darkened and its door slightly ajar. Without a word, she pushed the door open, her hand resting on the hilt of her sword. The interior was dimly lit, the flickering flame from a hearth casting long shadows on the walls. At the far end of the room, a figure sat alone at a table, cloaked in a dark hood. Verya's heart skipped a beat as she recognized the man immediately.

Ryle Thalor.

Her instincts told her everything she needed to know. The search for the shards had just taken a new turn.

# VI

# The Unseen Hand

The air in the library felt different now, even though Ryle had returned to the same place where everything had begun. It had only been a few days since he and Sarah had discovered the French Stone's shard, and already everything felt more charged, more dangerous. The words they had uncovered, the secrets they'd barely begun to understand—they hung in the air like smoke, threatening to choke them.

Ryle sat on the edge of one of the tall reading tables, staring at the maps and symbols they had spread out across the old parchment. The library was nearly empty at this hour, and the light streaming in from the late afternoon sun gave everything a golden, fragile glow. Despite the beauty of the place, Ryle couldn't shake the feeling that something was about to change—something beyond their control.

"Ryle?" Sarah's voice broke through his thoughts. She had been pacing the room, her brow furrowed as she scanned through old texts.

"Yeah?"

"We need help." She didn't pause, not even to glance at him. "We've hit a dead end here. These books... they're not giving us any more answers."

Ryle stood up, stretching his stiff muscles. "I know. But where are we going to find help? We're already on the edge of something. I don't trust anyone else."

Sarah stopped pacing and met his eyes. There was a flicker of something in her gaze—maybe doubt, maybe fear—but it was quickly replaced by the usual determination. "No, we don't need just anyone. We need someone who knows about the legends. Someone who has been around long enough to understand how these things work."

Ryle ran a hand through his hair, thinking. "Someone like... who?"

Sarah raised an eyebrow. "You remember Ethan?"

Ryle's stomach tightened at the mention of the name. Ethan was one of Sarah's old friends—a brilliant but eccentric tech genius who'd come to the university a few years ago. Ryle had met him a handful of times, and while Ethan had always struck him as a bit too obsessed with conspiracies and ancient myths, there was no denying his intellect.

"Ethan?" Ryle repeated, unsure. "You want to bring him into this?"

"Why not? He's got connections, he knows a lot about obscure myths, and—" She hesitated. "He owes me. He'll help."

Ryle frowned. "I don't like this, Sarah. He's... unpredictable."

"He's the best shot we've got," she said firmly. "Besides, we're not asking him to join us, just to point us in the right direction. It's all we can do."

Before Ryle could protest further, Sarah was already pulling out her phone and dialing a number. It rang twice before someone answered on the other end, and she spoke in low, urgent tones. Ryle could hear snippets of her conversation, but he was too lost in thought to focus on the details.

Ethan. He didn't trust him, but at this point, they didn't have many options. And if there was anyone who could shed light on the mysteries surrounding the French Stone and the Black Legion, it was probably him.

By the time Sarah hung up, Ryle had already moved to the window, staring out at the campus grounds. The shadows were lengthening as the sun dipped lower in the sky, and he couldn't shake the nagging feeling that something was about to unravel, something far beyond their control.

"We meet him at a café on Birch Street," Sarah said, breaking the silence. "He'll be waiting."

Ryle nodded but didn't turn around. "Fine. Let's just get this over with."

The café was small, tucked away in a quiet corner of the city. Its dim lighting and vintage decor made it feel like a place out of time. Ryle and Sarah entered through the narrow door, and the smell of freshly ground coffee hit them immediately. Ethan was already sitting at one of the tables, a large laptop open in front of him. He was hunched over, his fingers flying across the keyboard as though the world didn't exist outside his screen.

"Ethan," Sarah greeted, her voice calm and collected despite the tension that had begun to gather in the air.

Ethan didn't look up at first. His dark hair was messy, and he wore thick, round glasses that magnified his already large eyes. It took a moment for him to finish typing before he lifted his head and smiled, though it didn't quite reach his eyes.

"Well, well," he said, his voice light and almost too casual. "I thought it was you two. What brings you to my little corner of the world?"

"We need your help," Sarah said, her tone more serious than usual. She sat down across from him, and Ryle took a seat beside her. "It's about the French Stone."

Ethan's smile faltered, his fingers pausing over the keys. He looked between Sarah and Ryle, his expression unreadable.

"Ah, I see," he said, leaning back in his chair. "You've gotten yourselves into something far bigger than you expected, haven't you?"

"We've found a piece of it," Sarah continued, her voice steady. "We need to know more about the legends surrounding it. We need to understand what's happening."

Ethan's eyes narrowed slightly, and he pushed his glasses up the bridge of his nose. "And you think I'm the guy to help with that?"

Ryle stiffened, but Sarah gave him a subtle nudge, urging him to stay calm.

"You're the only one who knows anything about these myths," she said. "You've been researching this stuff for years."

Ethan studied them both for a long moment, then sighed. "Alright," he said, his tone shifting to something more serious. "I'll help you, but don't think I'm doing this out of the goodness of my heart. There are things you don't understand about this, things you shouldn't be poking around in."

"We don't have a choice," Ryle muttered, his patience wearing thin.

Ethan glanced at him sharply. "You don't even know what you're up against. This isn't just about a shard of some ancient stone. The Black Legion—"

"The Black Legion?" Ryle interrupted, his eyes flashing with recognition. "You know about them?"

Ethan smiled, but it was tight, forced. "I know more than you think. There's a reason they're called 'The Black Legion.' They're not just some secret society; they're part of something far older. Something dangerous."

"Then you'll help us," Sarah said, her voice gaining urgency. "You have to."

Ethan stared at the two of them, weighing his options. Finally, he nodded. "Fine. But you need to understand this—what you're messing with, it's not just history. It's power. And power always comes with a price."

Ryle clenched his fists under the table, feeling the weight of Ethan's words. There was something in his tone that made him uneasy. But they didn't have time to question it.

"We need to move fast," Sarah said. "What do we do next?"

Ethan tapped a few keys on his laptop, bringing up an ancient-looking map filled with symbols and cryptic notations.

"I've been tracking pieces of the French Stone for years," he said quietly. "And from what I've gathered, the Black Legion is more involved than we thought. They're not just searching for the shards—they're hunting them."

The tension in the air thickened as Ethan's words sank in. They weren't just facing a race against time. They were facing something far more dangerous: a shadowy group who had been hunting them all along.

And Ethan—Ryle wasn't so sure he could trust him.

But there was no turning back now. The pieces were in motion. The game had begun.

Later that evening, after the conversation had ended, Sarah and Ryle made their way back to the university, the weight of what they had learned pressing down on them. They hadn't spoken much on the walk back, both lost in their thoughts.

As they approached the steps of Harkstone, Ryle turned to Sarah. "Do you trust him?"

"Ethan?" she asked, glancing up at him. "I don't know. But we don't have any other choice."

Ryle hesitated, his gaze scanning the darkening campus. "What if he's leading us into something worse?"

"Then we deal with it when it happens," she said, her voice firm. "But right now, we don't have the luxury of waiting."

Ryle nodded, though doubt still lingered in his mind. As they climbed the stairs to the entrance, he couldn't shake the feeling that Ethan—just like the rest of them—was a player in a much larger game. A game with far higher stakes than they could even comprehend.

And somewhere in the shadows, the Black Legion was watching

The wind whipped through the trees as Ryle and Sarah entered the campus grounds, the weight of their decision bearing down on them. Ethan's words still hung in the air like a lingering fog. The Black Legion, he had said, was hunting them. But why? What could the Black Legion possibly want with a group of college students and a fractured shard of an ancient stone?

It didn't make sense.

Ryle ran a hand through his hair, his mind buzzing. He could feel the sharp edges of doubt scraping at the corners of his thoughts, gnawing away at the confidence he had managed to hold on to for so long. Ethan was hiding something—of that, Ryle was certain. The question was what?

"I still don't trust him," Ryle muttered, breaking the silence between them.

Sarah glanced at him, her pace steady. "I know. But we don't have many choices. He's the only one who's ever made any progress on this stuff."

"I don't care about progress, Sarah. I care about staying alive."

She stopped walking and turned to face him, her eyes serious. "I get it. But you have to trust me on this. I know Ethan. He's eccentric, but he's not a liar. He'll help us."

"But what if helping us means something worse?" Ryle shot back, his tone sharper than he intended. "What if he's using us?"

Sarah exhaled through her nose, her breath visible in the chilly evening air. "I don't know. But we're in this now. We can't turn back. And if there's one thing I know about Ethan, it's that he wants answers as much as we do. I'm not saying we trust him with our lives. But we need him. For now."

Ryle was about to respond when a voice called out behind them.

"Ryle! Sarah! Wait up!"

They both turned to see Ethan, jogging toward them, looking out of breath but determined. He had apparently followed them after their meeting, and he wasn't about to let them walk off without another word.

"Ethan?" Sarah said, raising an eyebrow. "What are you doing here?"

"Can't exactly let you two run off without me, can I?" he said, grinning slightly. "You're not the only ones who need answers, you know. I've been keeping tabs on the Black Legion, and I think it's about time we make some headway. If we're going to figure this out, we need to go to where they're based. Ashencliff."

Ryle's stomach twisted at the mention of Ashencliff. The ominous black cliffs that loomed in the distance, shrouded in dark secrets, had always been the stuff of legends. Everyone had heard the stories, but no one had ever been able to confirm what went on behind its cliffs. Even the most daring explorers who ventured close to the area never returned.

"We're not just walking into Ashencliff," Ryle said, his voice low. "You can't be serious. If the Black Legion's based there, it's not going to be some peaceful visit. It's a trap."

Sarah exchanged a glance with Ethan. "I agree. But we can't avoid it anymore. We don't have a choice."

Ethan nodded. "Exactly. The Black Legion isn't going to sit idly by while we figure out the pieces of the French Stone. We need to be proactive. If we can get to Ashencliff, maybe we can uncover more answers. They'll lead us right to the heart of the Legion."

Ryle stared at the two of them, his mind racing with conflicting thoughts. On one hand, the idea of going into the heart of enemy territory seemed like a death wish. On the other hand, he knew Sarah was right. They didn't have much of a choice. They had already stepped too far into the darkness to turn back now.

He took a deep breath and let it out slowly. "Alright," he said, his voice steady but filled with reluctant resolve. "Let's do this."

The journey to Ashencliff took the better part of the night. Ethan had insisted they take his old van—a beaten-up thing with stickers plastered all over the sides and the faint smell of stale coffee that had never quite left the upholstery. They drove in silence for hours, the road winding through dense forests and desolate fields. As they neared the outskirts of Ashencliff, the atmosphere grew heavier, darker. The air felt colder, almost unnatural, as if the very land itself had a malevolent presence.

By the time they reached the cliffs, it was well past midnight. The moon hung high in the sky, casting an eerie glow over the jagged rocks. Ashencliff wasn't just a place; it was a feeling. A looming shadow on the horizon, a place where the air itself seemed to hum with ancient, forgotten power. It felt wrong.

The van rolled to a stop near a grove of trees, just on the edge of the cliffs. Ethan killed the engine, and the three of them sat in silence, staring at the black rocks that rose from the earth like monstrous teeth.

"You sure about this?" Ryle asked, his voice barely more than a whisper.

"We don't have a choice," Sarah said, her tone firm.

Ethan opened the door and stepped out, stretching his arms. "Let's get this over with. I've mapped out some locations I think might be useful."

"Great," Ryle muttered, getting out of the van and slamming the door behind him. "Because I'm sure there's a treasure chest waiting for us."

"We're not looking for treasure," Sarah said, her voice laced with a quiet determination. "We're looking for answers."

They moved in silence through the trees, the path narrow and winding as it led them toward the cliffs. The ground beneath their feet was uneven, and the air smelled of damp earth and something else—something metallic. Ryle felt a chill crawl down his spine, but he didn't say anything. He couldn't help but feel like they were walking straight into a trap, that they were being watched by eyes that were older than time itself.

Ethan paused ahead of them, his hand raised as if signaling for them to stop. "This way," he said, his voice tight with excitement. "I've pinpointed a location nearby that could have the answers we need."

Ryle looked at Sarah, his expression unreadable. She nodded, her jaw set.

They followed Ethan deeper into the heart of Ashencliff, the ground becoming more unstable with each step. The cliffs loomed over them like silent, imposing sentinels, and the air seemed to hum with a low, vibrating energy that set Ryle's nerves on edge.

After what felt like hours of trekking through the thick underbrush, they came upon a small cave entrance hidden behind a cluster of rocks. It was easy to miss, almost too subtle to be a real entrance. But as Ethan knelt down and tugged at a hidden lever in the rock, the ground beneath them shifted, and the cave mouth opened wide.

"This is it," Ethan said, his voice tinged with excitement. "Whatever's in here, it's important."

Ryle stepped forward cautiously, his hand resting on the hilt of the dagger he had taken with him. The darkness of the cave seemed to swallow them whole as they ventured inside, the faint glow of Ethan's flashlight the only light guiding their way.

The deeper they went, the more oppressive the air became. The walls of the cave were lined with strange markings, symbols that didn't resemble anything Ryle had ever seen before. Some of them pulsed with a faint, unnatural light.

"Look at this," Sarah whispered, her voice barely audible. She was standing in front of a massive stone altar that sat in the center of a large cavern. It was covered in the same symbols, etched into the stone in jagged, almost violent strokes.

"This must be it," Ethan said, his voice almost reverent. "This is where they used to gather. The Black Legion."

Ryle stepped forward, his heart pounding in his chest. He had never been one for conspiracies, but as he gazed at the altar, he could feel it—a dark energy, a presence that lingered in the air, thick and suffocating.

"I don't like this," Ryle muttered, his instincts screaming at him to turn back.

But it was too late. They had already stepped into the heart of the darkness.

And it was waiting for them.

# VII

# The Hidden Secret

The air inside the cave was suffocating, thick with the weight of centuries-old secrets. The walls seemed to close in around them as Ryle, Sarah, and Ethan stood before the stone altar. The symbols etched into the dark stone pulsed faintly, like veins beneath a skin that no longer breathed. A sense of inevitability clung to the air, and Ryle couldn't shake the feeling that they were standing on the edge of something far darker than they realized.

Sarah was the first to move. She stepped cautiously toward the altar, her fingers grazing the surface of the stone. As she touched it, the markings seemed to shimmer, and a low hum reverberated through the cavern. Ryle instinctively stepped forward, his hand still on the hilt of his dagger. The sudden noise had made him uneasy, but Sarah didn't flinch.

"This place... It feels wrong," Ryle muttered, his eyes scanning the dark recesses of the cavern.

"I know," Sarah said, her voice distant, as though she were lost in thought. "But it's important. We need to understand what happened here."

Ethan, who had been quietly examining the far walls of the cave, turned to face them. "The Black Legion wasn't just a group of mercenaries or soldiers. They were scholars. They sought knowledge—power through understanding. This altar," he said, walking toward it, "wasn't built for sacrifices. It was a center of study. A place where they tapped into something—something far beyond anything we can comprehend."

Ryle didn't like the way Ethan's eyes shone with a strange fervor, like a man obsessed. "What do you mean, something beyond?"

Ethan ignored him and began muttering to himself, something in a language Ryle didn't understand. His voice was low and urgent, almost as if he were calling to something—or someone. As he spoke, the air around them thickened, and the low hum of the altar grew louder.

"Ethan, what are you doing?" Sarah asked, concern creeping into her voice.

"Trying to wake it," he said, his eyes never leaving the altar. "The Black Legion didn't just research ancient knowledge. They harnessed it. They used magic—power that has been hidden for centuries. If we can tap into it, we can learn everything. We'll have the power to stop the Black Legion—control the fate of the Shields and the Stone."

Ryle's stomach twisted with unease. This wasn't just about finding answers anymore. This was about control, about wielding something far more dangerous than they were ready for.

"I don't know, Ethan," Ryle said, his voice tight. "What if it's too much for us? What if it gets into our heads? You said they were scholars, but they also disappeared for a reason. Something went wrong."

Ethan's expression darkened. "Something did go wrong, yes. The Legion fell apart. But we don't have to make the same mistakes. We can learn from their failure."

Ryle's gaze flicked to Sarah, who was standing frozen, staring at Ethan with a mix of caution and disbelief. She knew something was off, too. But before either of them could speak, the altar began to rumble.

Ryle stumbled back as the stone cracked open, revealing a dark passage hidden beneath. The hum turned into a low, grinding noise that echoed through the cavern. A deep shadow swirled within the passage, like the heart of the darkness was finally waking up.

"Get back!" Ryle shouted, grabbing Sarah's arm and pulling her away from the altar. But she resisted.

"No. This is it," she said, her voice shaking. "This is what we've been looking for."

Before Ryle could argue, the shadow in the passage swirled violently, and a cold wind rushed out, sending them all stumbling backward. The cavern floor cracked open beneath them, as if the very earth was rejecting their intrusion. The air smelled of damp stone and something far more metallic—an iron-like tang that made Ryle's teeth itch.

Sarah stepped forward, her gaze fixed on the swirling shadow. "I can feel it," she whispered. "It's calling to me."

Ryle gripped her arm, pulling her back. "We're not going down there. Not without knowing what's waiting."

Ethan, meanwhile, had moved to the edge of the opening. His face was illuminated by the dim light of his flashlight, but there was something strange in his eyes—a glint of obsession, of something far darker than Ryle had ever seen.

"This is the Black Legion's legacy," Ethan said, his voice low and strained. "This is the power they wanted. This is the key to understanding everything."

The passage below them twisted and writhed like a living thing. Ryle couldn't shake the feeling that whatever lay ahead, it wasn't just some hidden chamber. This was a living, breathing force—ancient and hungry.

"Ethan!" Ryle shouted, his voice cracking. "Stop!"

But Ethan didn't stop. Instead, he moved forward, stepping into the passage. "This is our only chance," he muttered under his breath. "I have to do this. We all do."

Before Ryle could react, Ethan disappeared into the darkness below, swallowed whole by the shadow. His voice echoed back up, faint but urgent.

"I'm not leaving without answers."

Ryle stood there for a long moment, staring at the dark opening, the weight of their situation pressing down on him like a vice. His heart was racing, his breath coming in short gasps. He wanted to follow Ethan, but every instinct in his body told him to run—to get as far away from Ashencliff as possible before whatever ancient force waiting in the shadows consumed them all.

But Sarah didn't move. She stood frozen, staring at the darkness below with a look in her eyes that Ryle couldn't quite place.

"Sarah, don't," Ryle said, his voice low but desperate.

She turned to him, and for a brief moment, he saw something in her eyes—something unfamiliar. "Ryle... I don't know how to explain it. But I have to go down there. It's calling to me, too. This isn't just about the Stone. It's about understanding something much bigger. It's about... control."

"Control?" Ryle's voice rose with disbelief. "What are you talking about? We can't control this. We barely understand it. And neither does Ethan!"

She shook her head, her expression hardened. "But what if it's not just about survival anymore? What if we can use this power? What if we can change everything?"

Ryle grabbed her arm, desperation making his grip tight. "Sarah, listen to me. This is madness. I'm not letting you—"

"I'm going," she interrupted, her voice calm but firm. "I have to. And so do you."

Ryle's thoughts raced as he let go of her arm, his chest tightening. He knew she was right. There was no turning back now. They had crossed too many lines, uncovered too many secrets, to back out.

Swallowing his fear, Ryle stepped forward, following Sarah as she moved toward the opening in the ground. But as they approached, something in the air shifted—a low growl, a tremor in the earth beneath them. The darkness below seemed to pulse with life, drawing them in like a magnet.

And somewhere, deep in the shadows, Ethan's voice echoed back to them, as though mocking their hesitation.

"It's already too late."

Ryle stood at the edge of the gaping passage, staring into the abyss that seemed to breathe and shift like an entity in its own right. His heart pounded as he watched Sarah take another step forward, unhesitating. It was as if something had taken hold of her, pulling her deeper into the unknown. He could feel the pull too, but it was different for him. His instincts screamed at him to turn away, to walk back to the safety of the surface, where the air wasn't tainted by ancient, unknowable forces.

"Sarah, stop!" he shouted again, his voice laced with fear. But she didn't turn, didn't falter. She was resolute. Driven.

Ryle took a deep breath and stepped closer to her, his hand brushing against her arm, feeling the coldness that had settled into her skin.

"Sarah," he said again, softer now. "Please. This isn't us. This is a trap. Whatever lies down there... it's not something we can control."

She turned to him slowly, her expression unreadable, as though the world around her had fallen into a shadow of its own. "You don't understand, Ryle," she said quietly, her voice almost distant. "This isn't about control. This is about power. We're standing on the edge of something ancient, something that has been waiting for us to find it. We can't ignore it. We were meant to be here."

Ryle shook his head, his fingers tightening around his dagger. "Meant to be here? This isn't fate, Sarah. This is madness. We don't know what's down there. We're talking about the Black Legion's darkest secrets."

"But we know what's up here," she shot back, her eyes flashing. "The same thing we've always known: a half-finished story. Unanswered questions. This is the chance to finish it. To understand why everything has led us here. We can change everything."

Ryle swallowed hard. He wasn't sure if she was speaking out of conviction, or if something else had taken hold of her, something far deeper than they could see. The words felt too final, too absolute.

Before he could respond, there was a sudden flicker of movement below them. A low, guttural laugh echoed up from the depths, and the shadow in the passage seemed to grow, swallowing the light around it. Ryle's grip tightened on the dagger as the air grew thicker, the hum from the altar intensifying.

"We're not alone," Ryle muttered.

"I know," Sarah whispered, her voice barely audible now, as though she were speaking to herself. "But we never were, were we?"

There was a flash—sharp, blinding, and then the sound of something moving quickly, too quickly, through the air. Ryle's heart stopped as the shadow in the passage seemed to take shape, coalescing into something more solid. A figure, dark and shifting, appeared at the threshold of the stone cavern.

A pair of eyes—glowing faintly with an unnatural light—pierced the darkness, locking onto Ryle. The figure was tall, its form draped in tattered black robes. In its hand, it held a staff crowned with a jagged shard of stone, glowing with a faint, ominous energy. Its presence seemed to bend the very air around it, thickening it with power.

"Ethan..." Ryle breathed, recognition and fear intertwining in his voice.

Ethan's lips twisted into a grim smile, one that held no warmth, only cold certainty. "You shouldn't have come down here," he said, his voice carrying a strange edge, as if it were no longer entirely his own.

Ryle took a cautious step forward, his eyes never leaving Ethan. "What the hell happened to you?" he demanded. "What have you done?"

Ethan didn't answer immediately. Instead, he raised the staff, and the stone beneath their feet trembled in response. "I've done what I needed to do. What we all needed to do. The Black Legion's legacy is more than just history. It's a path. A path to power. A path to ascension."

Sarah's eyes flickered with something—curiosity, perhaps, or fear. "Ethan, this is madness," she said quietly.

"You can't seriously believe this is the answer. Look at you."

Ethan's gaze hardened, and he took a step toward them, the shadows swirling around him like a cloak. "I've seen the truth. I've heard it—whispered in the dark, in the blood of those who've come before us. This is where we were always meant to be. This power... it's not just about controlling the Shields. It's about shaping the world, bending it to our will."

Ryle stepped in front of Sarah, his hand on his dagger's hilt. "And what about us, Ethan? What about the people we care about? What about the world we're supposed to protect?"

Ethan's smile faltered for just a moment, his eyes flickering with something Ryle couldn't place. Then, as quickly as it had appeared, the moment passed, and Ethan's expression hardened once more. "The world we're supposed to protect? No. The world as it is—corrupt, broken, drowning in its own lies—needs to be remade. The Black Legion knew that. I know that now."

"Stop it, Ethan!" Ryle shouted, his voice rising with desperation. "This isn't you!"

"It is," Ethan replied, his voice cold, final. "It's always been me. The truth lies below, in the heart of this place. And it will be mine. All of it."

Without warning, he raised the staff high, and the ground beneath them cracked, sending a shockwave of energy through the air. Ryle staggered back, barely able to keep his balance as the cavern shook.

Sarah grabbed his arm, her grip strong. "Ryle, we need to get out of here—now!"

But Ryle didn't move. His eyes were locked on Ethan, who now stood at the center of the cavern, his form surrounded by a shifting mist of darkness and light. There was a pull, an undeniable force drawing Ryle toward him.

But his instincts screamed at him to run.

"Ethan, please!" Ryle yelled, his voice breaking. "This isn't you. You're being consumed by something—something you don't understand."

Ethan's eyes blazed with fury. "You've never understood, Ryle. You never will. You've always been too weak to see the truth."

Suddenly, the ground beneath them gave way. With a deafening roar, the earth cracked wide open, and the cavern began to collapse. Ryle and Sarah barely managed to leap back as chunks of stone and debris fell from the ceiling.

"We need to go!" Sarah screamed, pulling at Ryle's arm.

But Ethan didn't move. He stood in the center of the chaos, his eyes glowing with an unnatural light as the power of the Black Legion surged through him. "It's too late for you," he called out, his voice echoing through the cavern. "This world will be mine."

The shadow around him swelled, darkening the entire cavern. The last thing Ryle saw before they were forced to flee was Ethan's face—a mask of cold resolve as he raised the jagged shard of the French Stone high.

Then the ground split open beneath them, and Ryle and Sarah were plunged into darkness.

# VIII
# Omnagar

The wind howled across the plains of Omnagar, a relentless, biting force that carried with it the echoes of history—whispers of a time long forgotten. The city, once a beacon of civilization, now stood in ruin. Towering stone walls that had once marked the boundaries of the kingdom lay shattered and half-buried beneath layers of dust and time. The city's great spires, once soaring above the earth like the outstretched arms of gods, were now little more than jagged remains, their once-proud silhouettes barely visible against the ever-present gray sky.

Ryle stood at the edge of the ruins, his gaze sweeping across the desolate landscape. He had come here seeking answers, but in truth, he didn't know what he was looking for. The story of Omnagar had been told to him in fragments—bits and pieces passed down through myth, legend, and whispers. A city that had once been the heart of a mighty empire, now reduced to nothing more than a shadow of its former self.

There was something deeply unsettling about this place. Something that gnawed at the edges of his mind, pulling him deeper into the mystery of his own bloodline, his connection to the past. He could feel it—like a distant hum beneath the ground, a call that was almost imperceptible but undeniable. The weight of centuries pressed down on him, a reminder that he was standing where history had been made, where decisions had been forged in fire and blood.

Sarah stood beside him, her expression unreadable. The journey here had been long and arduous, but there was no turning back now. She had insisted on coming, as determined as ever to uncover the truth, even if it meant venturing into the heart of a forgotten kingdom. But Ryle could see it in her eyes—something had changed. The excitement, the hunger for knowledge that had once driven her, had been replaced with something else. Fear, maybe. Or something darker. He didn't know.

"This place..." Sarah murmured, her voice carrying the weight of a thousand unspoken thoughts. "It feels wrong, doesn't it?"

Ryle nodded, his throat tight. "Like it's alive. But not in the way we're used to."

They walked through the ruins, moving cautiously, the remnants of the city's grand architecture looming over them like silent sentinels. The stone streets, once bustling with life, were now cracked and broken, choked with weeds and debris. The only sounds were the wind and the distant creak of stones shifting beneath their feet.

As they ventured deeper into the heart of Omnagar, they found themselves drawn toward a massive structure—what was left of the Royal Citadel. The citadel had once been the seat of power for the rulers of Omnagar, a symbol of their might and authority. Now, it stood in ruins, its walls crumbling, its grandeur lost to the ravages of time.

Ryle felt the pull again, stronger this time, as they neared the entrance. There was something about this place—something that called to him, urging him forward. He could almost hear a voice in his mind, a soft whisper, urging him to enter. The air around the citadel felt thick, almost charged with an unseen energy. He could feel it in his bones.

"Ryle, wait," Sarah said, her voice tinged with caution. "Something's not right."

But Ryle was already moving, drawn toward the broken doors of the citadel. He pushed them open with a grunt, the ancient wood groaning in protest. Inside, the darkness was suffocating, but there was a faint light—dim, flickering—coming from deeper within. He could sense that it was drawing them in, just as the ruins of Omnagar had drawn them here.

"I can't explain it," Ryle said, turning to Sarah. "But I have to see what's inside."

Sarah hesitated, but then nodded, stepping forward. "We're in this together, remember?"

The interior of the citadel was like a tomb, silent and heavy with the weight of ages. The air was thick with dust, the floors littered with debris. Columns that once supported the great structure now lay shattered, their remnants scattered across the floor like the bones of giants. The walls were adorned with faded tapestries, their colors long since washed away, leaving behind only the faintest traces of what once was.

As they moved deeper into the citadel, the light grew stronger, guiding them toward a set of stairs that descended into the earth. Ryle's heart quickened. He knew, somehow, that whatever they were about to uncover lay beneath their feet.

"I don't like this," Sarah muttered, her voice tight with unease. "It feels like we're walking into something... something ancient."

Ryle didn't respond. He couldn't. His feet were already carrying him down the stairs, drawn by an unseen force. The air grew colder as they descended, the stone walls damp and slick with the moisture of forgotten centuries.

At the bottom of the stairs, they found themselves in a large, vaulted chamber. The ceiling arched high above them, supported by massive columns, their surfaces etched with intricate symbols and markings that seemed to pulse with an otherworldly energy. In the center of the room, a large pedestal stood, bathed in the dim light that seemed to emanate from nowhere and everywhere at once.

On the pedestal lay a stone—small, but unmistakable. The French Stone.

Ryle's breath caught in his throat. It was identical to the shard he had found beneath Harkstone University, the one that had pulsed with energy in his hand. The same cold, faintly glowing stone. But this one was whole, untouched, unbroken. And it seemed to call to him, louder now, almost as if it had been waiting for him to find it.

He reached out, his hand trembling as he took the stone in his palm. The moment his fingers brushed against it, a surge of energy coursed through him, filling him with a power he had never felt before. His vision blurred, and for a moment, he was no longer standing in the chamber. Instead, he was in another place—another time.

He saw the city of Omnagar in its prime, its people walking the streets, their lives full of promise and ambition. He saw the rulers of the city, proud and powerful, seated in their great hall, surrounded by advisors and scholars. But then, the vision shifted—darkness descended upon the city, the streets filled with fire and chaos. The rulers fell, their power shattered by a force they could not understand.

And then, he saw it—the Shield. The Black Shield, the one that had been used to protect the kingdom, now broken and corrupted. The stone had been used to create it, and in doing so, had brought the downfall of Omnagar.

Ryle gasped, dropping the stone back onto the pedestal. His mind reeled with the weight of the vision. This was the truth—the real truth—of what had happened to Omnagar. The city's destruction wasn't just a tale of greed and betrayal. It had been the result of the Shield, a power beyond anyone's control, a force that had turned against its creators.

"What did you see?" Sarah asked, her voice a whisper in the stillness of the chamber.

Ryle swallowed hard, his hands shaking. "Omnagar wasn't destroyed by war. It was destroyed by the Shield—the Black Shield. The stone was used to create it, and in doing so, it corrupted everything it touched."

Sarah stepped closer, her face pale. "So the Shield—it's connected to the Black Legion."

Ryle nodded, his mind still reeling. "It's all connected. The Black Legion, the Shields, Omnagar... It's all part of a cycle, a pattern that repeats itself over and over again."

Sarah's eyes darkened. "Then we need to stop it. Whatever it is, whatever's coming next, we can't let it happen again."

Ryle looked down at the French Stone, still glowing faintly on the pedestal. He felt its power pulsing through him, calling him, urging him to take it. And for the first time, he realized something: he wasn't just a bystander in this story. He was part of it.

He was part of the legacy of Omnagar.

And the fate of the world rested in his hands.

Ryle could feel the weight of the moment pressing on him, the enormity of what lay before him almost suffocating. The stone at the pedestal pulsed, its faint glow echoing the rhythm of his own heartbeat. As he stood there, Sarah's voice broke through the thick silence in the chamber, but it sounded distant—almost as though it were coming from the edge of a dream.

"Ryle... what do we do now?" she asked, her tone laced with both uncertainty and determination. She was always so confident, but in this place, under the oppressive weight of its history, even Sarah seemed unsure.

He stared at the stone, his fingers still tingling from the brief contact with it. The images he'd seen, the visions of Omnagar in its prime, the rulers, the betrayal, and the corruption, swirled in his mind like storm clouds. He didn't have the answers—not yet—but he knew one thing for sure: they had to stop the cycle. The Black Shield, the French Stone, the Black Legion—they were all connected, tied together in ways that only the past could reveal.

"I don't know," Ryle admitted. "But I think we need to go deeper. There's more to this place—more to Omnagar than we realize. The stone... the Shield... it's all a part of something bigger."

Sarah nodded, her brow furrowed in thought. "We can't let it happen again. Whatever it was that destroyed this place, we can't let it take hold of the world again. We're not just here to find answers anymore, are we?"

Ryle shook his head slowly. "No. We're here to stop it. To break the cycle."

The weight of their mission hung between them like an invisible chain. It was a responsibility that neither of them had asked for, yet they both knew it was theirs now. They had come to Omnagar seeking the truth, but what they had found was something far darker—something that had the potential to unravel everything.

Sarah stepped forward, her eyes scanning the chamber. "There must be something here, something more we're missing. This place can't just be a tomb. It feels... like a warning."

A chill ran down Ryle's spine as he followed her gaze. The symbols etched into the columns surrounding the room seemed to shift, their meanings elusive. He could almost hear them whispering, the ancient words beckoning him to listen, to understand.

He moved toward one of the columns, running his fingers over the worn carvings. There was a sense of recognition in the shapes, a connection to the visions he'd seen. As his hand traced the patterns, he felt a subtle vibration in the stone beneath his fingertips, as though the column itself were alive, aware.

Suddenly, a low rumble echoed through the chamber, followed by the unmistakable sound of grinding stone. Ryle's heart skipped a beat as the wall opposite them began to shift, revealing a hidden passageway. The air in the room grew colder, and for a moment, everything seemed to freeze—time itself holding its breath.

"What the hell..." Sarah murmured, her voice barely a whisper. "How did that happen?"

Ryle took a step forward, his curiosity piqued. "I don't know. But I think we're meant to go through there."

Before Sarah could respond, a voice, deep and resonant, filled the chamber. The words seemed to come from everywhere at once, reverberating off the walls, echoing in Ryle's chest.

"You seek the truth, but be warned," the voice boomed. "The path to knowledge is fraught with peril. Only those who are truly worthy may pass."

Ryle froze. The voice was unlike anything he had ever heard. It wasn't a physical sound—it seemed to resonate within him, like an ancient echo of the past.

"Who are you?" he demanded, his voice shaky, yet steady. "What do you want?"

The response came as a low, rumbling laugh. "I am no one. But I am everyone. I am the past, the present, and the future. I am the power that lies beneath this city, the one that you have awakened."

Ryle's mind raced. The voice... it wasn't just a warning. It was a presence—something old, something vast. It wasn't merely an echo of the past; it was an active force, a living testament to the legacy of Omnagar.

Sarah's grip on her flashlight tightened. "Ryle, what is this? We have to leave. This feels wrong."

But Ryle stood rooted in place, staring at the opening before him. He could feel the pull—the same pull that had brought him here in the first place, the one that had led him to the French Stone, to the broken city of Omnagar.

"No," he said firmly. "We have to go forward. We've come this far. We're not turning back now."

With a hesitant nod, Sarah reluctantly followed him as they stepped through the darkened archway, the stones beneath their feet cool and smooth. The passageway was narrow, winding down at a steep angle, the walls lined with the same ancient carvings they had seen in the chamber above. The further they descended, the darker it became, until even their flashlight was no match for the oppressive blackness that seemed to consume everything.

They walked in silence for what felt like an eternity, each step taking them deeper into the heart of the ruins. The air grew thick, heavy with an ancient power that pressed in on them from all sides. Every now and then, Ryle would catch glimpses of something moving in the shadows—flickers of motion, like the remnants of long-forgotten souls, trapped in the dark.

Finally, they reached the end of the passage, where a large, circular chamber awaited them. At the center stood a massive stone altar, surrounded by broken statues, their faces worn and eroded by time. The altar was adorned with strange symbols, similar to those on the columns above. But there was something else—something that drew Ryle's gaze like a magnet.

Atop the altar lay another stone. Not the French Stone this time, but something far darker—something that seemed to pulse with an ominous energy.

It was the Black Shield.

Ryle felt a shiver run down his spine. The Black Shield—the object that had been tied to the downfall of Omnagar, the object that had corrupted the kingdom and led to its ruin. It lay there before him, waiting, as if it had been waiting for him all this time.

"Ryle... this is it," Sarah whispered, her voice trembling. "This is what we've been looking for."

Ryle stepped forward, his hand trembling as he reached toward the stone. As his fingers brushed the surface of the Black Shield, a surge of energy coursed through him, more powerful than anything he had ever experienced. His vision blurred, and the world around him seemed to shift and warp. He was no longer in the chamber with Sarah. Instead, he was standing in a vast, empty expanse, a void that stretched on forever.

And then, before him, the figure of a man appeared.

Tall, imposing, and clad in black armor, the man stood as if he had materialized from the darkness itself. His face was hidden beneath a hood, but Ryle could feel the weight of his gaze, the crushing presence that emanated from him like a storm on the horizon.

"Varek," Ryle whispered, his voice barely audible.

The figure nodded, though his face remained hidden. "You have come far, Ryle Thalor," the voice echoed, low and commanding. "But you have not yet seen the full extent of the power you seek."

Ryle stepped back, his heart pounding in his chest. "What do you want from me? What is this power?"

The figure raised a hand, and the air around Ryle seemed to freeze. "The Black Shield is more than just an object of power," Varek said. "It is a gateway. A portal to a power far greater than you can comprehend. And it is through this power that you will fulfill your destiny. The question is—will you embrace it?"

Ryle's mind raced. He had come this far to find the truth, to stop the cycle, but what if the truth was something far darker than he had ever imagined? What if the only way to end the chaos was to join it?

The Black Shield pulsed in his hand, urging him forward. And for a brief moment, he considered it. The power, the answers, the legacy of Omnagar—it was all within his grasp.

But then, as quickly as it came, the moment passed. He took a deep breath, forcing himself to push away the fear and temptation that threatened to overtake him. He could not—would not—let the darkness take hold.

"We won't let you win," Ryle said, his voice firm, resolute.

Varek's laugh echoed through the void, cold and without mercy. "We shall see, Ryle Thalor. We shall see."

And with that, the vision faded, and Ryle was back in the chamber, standing beside Sarah, the Black Shield still resting on the altar before them.

"We need to get out of here," Ryle said urgently, his voice shaky but determined. "We've uncovered enough for now."

Sarah nodded, though there was something in her eyes that told Ryle she had felt the same pull, the same temptation. They turned and left the chamber, their footsteps echoing through the hollow halls of Omnagar, but Ryle knew one thing for certain:

The battle was only just beginning.

# IX

# The Echoes of Omnagar

The sun was setting as Ryle and Sarah made their way back through the ruins of Omnagar. The once-great city now lay in silence, a shadow of its former self. The air was thick with the weight of its history, a history that had been buried beneath layers of time, dust, and forgotten dreams. Every step they took seemed to stir the very stones beneath their feet, the echo of past footsteps reverberating in their minds.

Ryle's fingers still tingled from his contact with the Black Shield. The vision he had seen—Varek, the man in black armor, the power that lay beyond the shield—kept replaying in his mind. He couldn't shake the feeling that they were on the precipice of something far larger than they had ever anticipated. The answers they sought were within reach, but the closer they came, the more the darkness pressed against them.

"Ryle," Sarah said, breaking the silence. "You've been quiet ever since... well, since the Black Shield."

Ryle glanced over at her, his expression tense. "I can't stop thinking about it. The power—it's like it's calling to me, pulling at something inside me."

"Do you think it's part of what's happening to you? The connection to Omnagar? The bloodline?" Sarah asked, her voice soft but full of concern. "I mean, the way it felt when you touched it—it was almost like it recognized you."

He nodded slowly. "I felt it too. Like I'm tied to it in some way, but I don't know how. Varek said the Black Shield is a gateway. A way to unlock something greater, something... dangerous."

"Maybe we need to stop before we get too far into it," Sarah suggested, her tone hesitant. "Whatever this is, it's bigger than us. And I don't think we can control it. Maybe we should go back. Warn someone. Get help."

Ryle shook his head. "We can't. Not yet. There's too much at stake. I don't even know who we could trust at this point. But we can't let the Black Legion or whoever else is after the Shield get their hands on it."

"Do you really think the Black Legion is involved in this?" Sarah asked, her voice wary. "I mean, we've heard of them, but... I don't know. They're dangerous. And if they're connected to Varek, then things are already worse than we thought."

Ryle clenched his fists, feeling the weight of their situation pressing down on him. "Yes, I think they're involved. Varek wouldn't have shown up if it were just about the Shield. He has a plan, and it's connected to the Black Legion. They've been waiting for something like this for years. They want the Shield, and they'll stop at nothing to get it."

The sun dipped below the horizon, casting long shadows across the desolate landscape. The remnants of Omnagar loomed ahead, the once-mighty towers now crumbling ruins, their sharp edges silhouetted against the fiery sky. It was a city that had once been filled with life, with power, but now it was a tomb, a monument to the hubris of its rulers.

And yet, as they continued their journey through the remnants of Omnagar, Ryle couldn't shake the feeling that something was watching them. The air felt heavy, as though the very city itself was alive, holding its breath, waiting for something to happen.

"Do you hear that?" Sarah whispered, her voice barely audible.

Ryle stopped in his tracks, his heart skipping a beat. He strained his ears, but all he could hear was the distant sound of wind rustling through the ruined city. There was nothing else. No footsteps. No voices.

"I don't hear anything," Ryle said, trying to keep his voice steady.

Sarah shook her head, her eyes scanning the horizon. "No, listen. There's something—just beyond the walls. It's faint, but I swear I can hear it. Like... whispers."

Ryle felt a chill run down his spine. The whispers. They had been there before. In the chamber beneath the library. In the dreams that had haunted him since the first moment he had touched the French Stone.

Without saying a word, he grabbed Sarah's arm, pulling her toward a nearby crumbling wall. They crouched low, trying to remain hidden. Ryle's mind raced as he tried to make sense of what was happening. The city of Omnagar, the Black Shield, the Black Legion—everything was converging on them. And he had a terrible feeling that whatever was lurking just beyond the walls was a part of it.

The whispers grew louder, and Ryle's breath caught in his throat. They were unmistakable now, a low, guttural sound, like voices from the past, coming from somewhere deep within the ruins.

Suddenly, the ground beneath them trembled. A low rumble shook the earth, followed by the sound of stone grinding against stone. Ryle's eyes widened as a massive section of the wall nearby slid open, revealing a hidden passage. A dark, foreboding tunnel that seemed to stretch endlessly into the heart of the city.

Before Ryle could react, a figure emerged from the shadows. Tall, cloaked in darkness, the figure moved with the grace of a predator—silent, swift, and deadly. Ryle's hand instinctively went to his side, reaching for the knife he had tucked into his belt. But before he could draw it, the figure spoke.

"I've been waiting for you," the voice was smooth, like velvet, but laced with a cold edge that sent a shiver down Ryle's spine.

"Who are you?" Ryle demanded, trying to steady his breath.

The figure stepped forward, his face emerging from the shadows. It was a man, with dark eyes that seemed to glimmer with malice. His features were sharp, angular—an unsettling smile playing at the corners of his lips. He was dressed in a dark cloak, the fabric swirling around him like a living thing.

"I am no one," the man said, his voice low and confident. "But you... you are Ryle Thalor, aren't you?"

Ryle's eyes narrowed. "What do you want?"

The man chuckled softly, the sound sending a wave of unease through Ryle's chest. "I want what is mine. The Black Shield, the power that it holds. And you, Ryle, you are the key to unlocking it."

Sarah moved closer to Ryle, her hand brushing his. "We don't know what you're talking about," she said, her voice steady but laced with fear. "We're just trying to figure out what happened here. What happened to Omnagar."

The man's smile grew wider, more sinister. "Omnagar fell because it was weak. Because it was corrupt. But now, it is reborn. And you, Ryle, you are the one who will bring it back to its full power. The Black Shield has chosen you."

Ryle's blood ran cold. "You're lying. I won't help you."

The man's expression hardened, his eyes narrowing into slits. "You don't have a choice. The Shield has already chosen you. And soon, you will understand."

Without warning, the figure raised his hand, and a wave of dark energy erupted from him, sending Ryle and Sarah crashing to the ground. The world around them spun, darkness consuming their vision as they struggled to rise.

Ryle fought to stay conscious, his head spinning. The whispers grew louder, the voices of Omnagar's past closing in on them. And in the distance, he could hear something else—a sound that sent a chill of terror through him.

Footsteps.

Heavy, measured footsteps, echoing through the ruins of the city.

"Get up," Sarah hissed, her grip on Ryle's arm firm. "We need to run."

But as they struggled to their feet, the figure in the shadows stepped forward, blocking their path. And with a voice that resonated with ancient power, he spoke again.

"The Black Legion is coming. And so is the Master."

Ryle's pulse raced as he fought to stand, feeling the weight of the dark energy still swirling around them like a storm. The figure, cloaked in shadows, stood before them like an immovable wall. His smile twisted with something dark, something that felt ancient, malevolent. Ryle's fingers gripped the hilt of his knife, but it felt like a useless weapon in the face of the raw power emanating from this stranger.

"Get back!" Sarah shouted, pulling Ryle behind her, her voice filled with a fierce urgency. "We don't have time for this!"

The figure didn't flinch, his gaze locking onto Ryle as if he were reading the very core of his being. "You still don't understand, do you? You are the bridge between the old world and the new. The Shield chose you, Ryle Thalor. And now you must choose: remain in the shadows or embrace what you were always meant to be."

Ryle shook his head, trying to clear the fog that had clouded his thoughts. He wanted to deny everything he had learned, to refuse the path that seemed to stretch out before him. But deep down, a small part of him knew it was too late for that. Whatever this Shield was, whatever power it held—it was already inside him.

"I won't join you," Ryle said, his voice firmer now, though doubt lingered in his heart. "I won't let you use me."

The figure's smile deepened, but there was no amusement in it—only coldness, and something much darker. "You don't have a choice. The Master's will is inevitable. You will come to understand. The Shield is not just a weapon. It is a key. And in the end, you will unlock its true power."

Ryle felt something stir inside him. It was a sharp, undeniable pull—something calling him, beckoning him toward the figure before him. He recoiled, trying to shut out the feeling, but it was like trying to ignore a voice in his head. The Shield was not just an object—it was alive. And it wanted him.

"Ryle!" Sarah's voice broke through the haze, sharp and insistent. She grabbed his arm and pulled him backward, toward the remnants of the city's walls. "We have to go. Now."

But before they could make their move, the air around them shifted. A low rumble vibrated the ground beneath them, followed by a sharp crack—a sound like thunder. The earth trembled as if it were waking from a long slumber, and the city itself seemed to groan under the weight of something ancient stirring.

The figure took a step toward them, his hand raised. "You think you can run from this? You cannot escape what has already been set in motion. The Black Legion will find you. And when they do, you will have no choice but to submit to your fate."

Suddenly, there was a flash of light—a blinding, white light that filled the ruined city. Ryle shielded his eyes, his heart pounding in his chest as the world seemed to ripple and shift around him. The figure staggered back, his hand shielding his face from the light. But it wasn't just any light. It felt... like the Shield reacting to something.

And then, as quickly as it had come, the light faded, leaving behind a silence so complete it felt like the city had been hollowed out. The rumbling stopped, the tension that had gripped Ryle's chest released, but in its place, there was only the feeling of something—something vast—lingering in the air.

"What the hell was that?" Sarah whispered, her voice thick with disbelief.

Ryle didn't answer right away. His mind was reeling from the sudden surge of energy, from the overwhelming sensation that he had just narrowly escaped something he didn't fully understand. He turned to look at the figure, but the stranger was already retreating into the shadows of the crumbling city, his form blending with the darkness as if he were part of it.

For a long moment, there was nothing but the eerie stillness of Omnagar. But Ryle could feel it—the threat, the danger still hanging in the air. The Black Legion was coming. The Master was coming. And there was no way to avoid what was coming next.

"We need to get out of here," Ryle said, his voice tight with urgency. "Now."

Sarah didn't hesitate. She grabbed his hand and pulled him toward the nearest path leading out of the ruins. But as they turned to leave, Ryle paused for just a moment, his eyes scanning the city one last time. Something in the distance—something deep within the heart of Omnagar—called to him, beckoning him toward it. The power of the Shield was undeniable, and it was beginning to stir within him, urging him to go deeper, to seek out the source of that call.

But he didn't know if he could trust it. He didn't know if he could trust anything anymore.

"Ryle," Sarah said, her voice softer now. "We don't have time to wait. If we're going to survive this, we need to leave before they find us."

Ryle nodded, snapping out of his reverie. He turned away from the city's heart and followed Sarah as she led the way. But as they emerged from the shadows of Omnagar, the sense of unease didn't lift. It only grew stronger. The Black Legion was out there. And they wouldn't stop until they had the Shield.

The journey ahead would be one of survival—of trying to outpace fate, to escape a past that refused to stay buried. But as the city faded behind them, one thing was certain:

they were no longer just running from their enemies. They were running from the past—and the power that had been waiting for them all along.

As Ryle and Sarah made their way back toward the last place they had camped, the night seemed to stretch on forever. The wind whispered across the hills, carrying with it the weight of ancient secrets, of things forgotten long ago. Omnagar had been the birthplace of the Black Shield, but it had also been the birthplace of something far more dangerous: the Master, Varek, and the dark legacy that was awakening once more.

Behind them, in the ruins of Omnagar, the echoes of the past stirred once again. The whispers, the shadows, and the power that had once ruled the city—they were all rising, and they would not rest until the Shield was theirs.

And Ryle had no idea just how much of the past he was carrying with him.

# X

# The Master of The Shields

fThe cold wind swept across the ruined landscape, carrying with it the faintest taste of salt and earth. Ryle stood at the edge of a cliff, staring out at the vast expanse of the sea below. The sky was dark, with the moon hidden behind thick clouds, casting an almost tangible weight over the land. The silence of the world around him felt suffocating—heavy, as if the past itself had come alive and now watched them in the shadows.

Behind him, Sarah was busy checking their supplies, organizing their next move, but Ryle couldn't focus on any of it. His thoughts kept returning to the same place—the ruins of Omnagar. The city, abandoned but never forgotten, and the ominous figure he had encountered in its heart. The one who had spoken of the Master.

Varek.

The name rang through his mind like a bell tolling in the distance. The more he thought about it, the more unsettled he became. The encounter in Omnagar hadn't been just a warning—it had been a summons. A summons to a destiny that had been waiting for him longer than he could comprehend.

The Master of the Shields.

He didn't even know what that title meant, but somehow, he understood the gravity of it. The Master was not just some ancient tyrant, a distant figure from a lost time. No, Varek was something far more dangerous—he was the key to the darkness, the force that had shaped the world of the Shields and the Black Legion. The story of Omnagar, of the Shields themselves, was twisted, buried under layers of myth, but the core truth of it was clear: Varek was the origin of all things broken.

"Ryle."

Sarah's voice broke through his thoughts, her tone soft yet heavy with an unspoken weight. She had noticed his distance, his restless energy. She always did.

He turned to face her, the unease still gnawing at the edges of his mind. "I can't stop thinking about Omnagar," he admitted. "About Varek. That place—there's something calling me. It's like I was meant to be there."

She stepped closer, her brow furrowed. "It's not safe. We've been running from the Black Legion for weeks now. And every time we think we're safe, something else drags us deeper into this madness. You're not meant to be a part of it, Ryle. You know that, don't you?"

He didn't know.

He wasn't sure of anything anymore. The more he learned about the Shields, the more he realized how little he understood about himself. He wasn't just a bystander. This—whatever it was—was happening to him. The Shield, the piece he carried, wasn't just an object. It was part of him. It was awakening a side of him he didn't recognize. The ancient power, the legacy of Omnagar, was in his blood. And the more he fought it, the more it seemed to take root.

But it wasn't just the Shield that called to him. It was Varek. The Master of the Shields.

"There's more I need to know," Ryle said, his voice raw with determination. "We can't outrun it forever, Sarah. We need answers."

Sarah didn't respond immediately. Instead, she studied him, her gaze searching, as if weighing the choice before them. Finally, she sighed, dropping her gaze to the ground. "Fine. But we do this my way. We find a safe place to hide, gather more information, and then we confront whatever this is. I won't let you walk into the heart of this without knowing what we're up against."

"Agreed," Ryle said. "But I'm not sure we have much time left. The Black Legion will find us sooner or later. And when they do, they'll have more than just soldiers on their side. They'll have Varek. And that's something none of us can outrun."

That night, they camped beneath the shrouded trees of a forgotten forest, far from the shores of Omnagar but close enough for Ryle to feel the pull of its ancient past. The moon was barely visible through the clouds, but the wind carried a chill that spoke of impending storms. The world felt pregnant with a threat they could almost taste.

As Ryle lay awake, staring up at the canopy, he couldn't shake the image of Varek—the Master of the Shields.

The legend was simple, but the implications were far darker. Omnagar had once been the heart of an empire, a city of unmatched power, built upon the foundations of the Shields—ancient artifacts forged with unimaginable power. But the empire had fallen. Betrayed. Destroyed. And

Varek, the leader of the Shields, had been at the center of it all.

Varek had been a man, once—a brilliant tactician, a leader of armies, a protector of his people. He had fought for his kingdom with unmatched skill, but something had broken inside him. They say it was power, greed, or the torment of his own mind. But whatever it was, it had twisted him into something more than human.

He had betrayed those closest to him, causing the downfall of Omnagar and the collapse of the empire. And then, with the destruction of the kingdom, the Shields had scattered. They were broken, hidden, and scattered across the world, leaving only whispers of their existence behind.

But that wasn't the end of Varek.

The Master had become something else. Something darker.

The Master of the Shields was no longer a man. He had transcended his mortality, become part of the darkness itself. His name had become a curse, an echo of something far older and far more terrifying than any of them could comprehend.

Varek had learned to harness the power of the Shields—not just as a weapon, but as a means of controlling minds, bending souls to his will. He had become an immortal specter, a force that could manipulate the very fabric of the world around him. And now, his legacy lived on in the Black Legion, in the search for the Shield's power that would restore his full reign.

The Masters of the Shields weren't just leaders—they were cursed, bound to the artifacts they wielded, and that curse had passed to the one who was destined to wield the final Shield: Ryle.

And Varek's influence? It had never truly ended. He had lived on in the Black Legion, a network of power-hungry followers who sought to revive his reign. The Legion was growing stronger, and with each passing day, it seemed as if they were closing in on the remnants of the Shields.

Ryle knew it now. The Shield he carried wasn't just a weapon—it was the key to something far greater, something far more dangerous.

As the night stretched on, Ryle's mind began to swirl with the weight of it all. He could hear the whispers again, the call of the Shield in his mind, urging him toward something. It wasn't clear what it wanted, but he could feel it—this was no longer a choice of good or evil. It was a fight for survival.

And Varek? He would stop at nothing to reclaim what he had lost.

The Master of the Shields had returned.

And Ryle was about to face him.

The dawn broke cold, the pale light filtering through the dense trees above them like fractured glass. Ryle rose slowly, stretching his stiff limbs, the remnants of sleep still clinging to him. Sarah was already packing their things, her movements efficient but sharp, as if the events of the past few days had worn her thin. They both knew that their next steps could determine everything.

Ryle glanced back toward the horizon, toward the looming shadow of Omnagar in the distance, waiting for them. It was more than just a city; it was a tomb. And somewhere in its wreckage, buried deep within its forgotten halls, lay the truth they both sought.

He swallowed hard, his thoughts still entangled in the legend of Varek, the Master of the Shields. He had always been taught that the past was buried for a reason—that some stories were best left forgotten. But now, he understood. The past wasn't just a memory; it was a prison. A trap. A curse.

And it had followed him here.

"We need to move," Sarah said, her voice flat, as she stood up, dusting her hands off on her worn jacket. She didn't look at him directly, as if afraid of what she might see in his eyes. "We need to get to Omnagar before the Black Legion finds us."

Ryle nodded without speaking. He felt the weight of the Shield at his side, heavy, pulling him toward an inevitable confrontation. His hand instinctively reached for the shard of the French Stone, still nestled in his pocket. Its power had been growing stronger with each passing day, its pulse steady, almost synchronized with his heartbeat. He wasn't sure what it wanted from him, but he knew one thing—it was connected to Varek, to the Shields, and to everything that had happened long before his birth.

"Are you sure about this?" Sarah asked, her gaze finally meeting his. "I'm not talking about getting to Omnagar—I'm talking about what happens when we get there. We don't know what we'll find."

"I don't think we have a choice anymore," Ryle said, voice hoarse. "Varek is real. And the Black Legion is getting closer. They're looking for the Shield. They're looking for me. If we don't stop them, everything will fall apart."

Sarah didn't argue. She didn't need to. The determination in his voice had become its own kind of truth.

They gathered the rest of their supplies quickly, and without further words, began their trek toward Omnagar.

The path to the ruined city took longer than Ryle had anticipated. The landscape became more barren as they moved closer, the trees thinning out into jagged rocks and broken earth. Every step forward felt like a step backward, as if the very land was pushing them away from their destination. He couldn't shake the feeling that something was watching them—something ancient and malevolent.

By midday, they stood on the edge of the city, looking down at what was left of Omnagar. Once a sprawling metropolis of golden spires and great halls, the city was now little more than a crumbling ruin. The once-proud buildings had collapsed, leaving only fractured stone and scattered debris in their wake. It was hard to tell where the city had begun and where the earth had swallowed it whole. The ground itself seemed to pulse with an unsettling energy, as if Omnagar's destruction hadn't been enough to silence it.

"Let's get inside," Sarah said quietly, her voice edged with a tension Ryle could feel in his own bones. She turned away, leading the way down a narrow, winding path that cut through the rubble.

Ryle followed without hesitation, his eyes scanning the ruins. His heart was pounding in his chest, each beat louder than the last. He wasn't sure if it was fear or anticipation or something darker that was causing it, but he couldn't ignore it.

The further they went, the more he felt the weight of the place pressing in on him. It wasn't just the destruction—it was the memory. Omnagar had been a place of power, of knowledge. The Shields had been created here, and Varek had ruled it all.

They found the entrance to the city's ancient library, a once-grand structure whose pillars were now little more than fractured stone. The doors had long since rotted away, but the archway still stood, half-sunken into the earth. It felt like they were stepping into the belly of a beast, its carcass decaying but still holding something vital.

Inside, the air was thick with dust, and the silence was oppressive. The shelves that had once held priceless knowledge were now bare, their books long since lost or destroyed. But in the center of the room, amidst the rubble, there was something Ryle had not expected to find—a pedestal.

It stood alone, bathed in a faint, unnatural light that seemed to come from nowhere. On the pedestal rested a single object: a shield.

Ryle's breath caught in his throat as he stepped forward, almost as if drawn by an invisible force. This was no ordinary shield. It was old—ancient, in fact. The metal was tarnished, its edges worn with age, but there was no mistaking it. It was one of the Shields.

One of the Broken Shields.

The realization hit him with the force of a blow. The object before him wasn't just a relic—it was the key. The Shield that had once belonged to Varek. The one that had been lost with Omnagar.

He reached out instinctively, fingers trembling as they brushed against the cool metal. The moment he touched it, a surge of energy coursed through him, making his head spin. Visions flashed before his eyes—flashes of Omnagar in its prime, soldiers marching under banners of black, the sound of battle, of screams. And then, the face of a man.

Varek.

The vision lasted only a moment, but it was enough to send Ryle stumbling back, his hand clutching his chest as the energy from the Shield faded.

"That's it," Sarah whispered, her voice barely audible. "That's what they've been looking for."

"Not just this," Ryle said, still shaking from the vision. "It's part of something bigger. I felt it—the Shield... it's calling me."

Before Sarah could respond, a sound broke the silence—the faintest echo of footsteps.

"Ryle," she warned, her voice tight with fear. "We're not alone."

Ryle turned sharply, his heart hammering in his chest. From the shadows of the ruined library, figures emerged—figures clad in black, their faces obscured by dark hoods. The Black Legion.

They had found them.

"Leave now, or you will die where you stand," a voice called out from the darkness. It was cold, calculated—like steel cutting through the air.

Ryle's hand went instinctively to the Shield at his side, the weight of it now a burden he couldn't ignore. He glanced at Sarah, and in that instant, he knew.

There was no turning back.

The Master of the Shields had returned

# XI

# The Broken Shields

The ground beneath Ryle's feet trembled, the weight of the Black Legion's presence pressing in on him like a vice. The shield in his hand, now warm to the touch, pulsed with a subtle, almost imperceptible rhythm. It felt like a heartbeat—like the city itself was alive, waiting for him to unlock its secrets. But Ryle couldn't focus on that now.

The Legion was here.

His mind raced, racing between the Shield in his hand and the threat looming in the shadows. He looked toward Sarah, whose hand was resting on her knife, eyes scanning the darkened ruins of Omnagar's library. The Black Legion would not hesitate. They had never been merciful, and their reach had only grown since the fall of the city.

"You know what they want," Sarah said, her voice low but sharp with urgency. "They're after the Shield. And they're not here for anything else."

Ryle nodded, fingers tightening on the metal of the Shield. He could feel its power seeping into him, melding with his heartbeat. "It's not just about the Shield," he said, his voice steady despite the fear gnawing at his insides. "It's about the city. Omnagar... it's all connected. The Shields... Varek... everything."

As if on cue, a dark figure stepped forward, emerging from the shadows of the ruined library. The man was cloaked in a flowing black robe, his face obscured by the hood. But the voice that came from beneath the hood was unmistakable.

"You are right," the voice said, cold and commanding, as if the speaker had always known Ryle's every thought. "It's never been just about the Shield. It's about what Omnagar once was—and what it still is."

Ryle's heart raced. "Who are you?" he demanded, his grip tightening on the Shield. It felt like it was drawing power from him, feeding off his fear and uncertainty. But that wasn't enough. He needed answers.

"I am the one who remembers," the figure replied. "I have waited for this moment since the fall of Omnagar, since the day the Master of the Shields fell. I have watched you. All of you."

The figure's cloak billowed as he took a step closer, his footsteps echoing in the quiet space. Ryle could sense something ancient in his presence, something that went beyond human understanding. A coldness that didn't belong to the world of the living. The man's aura felt as old as the city itself.

"I have lived through centuries," the figure continued. "Omnagar was not merely a city. It was a sanctuary. A place of power, built upon the shields that guarded not just the kingdom, but the very fabric of this world. The Shields were not just weapons—they were anchors. Anchors to hold the forces of chaos at bay."

"The Shields...?" Ryle repeated, his mind reeling. "What do you mean? I thought they were destroyed."

"Destroyed?" The figure's laughter was hollow, devoid of humor. "You think destruction can erase something that powerful? No. The Shields were broken, scattered, and hidden—far from the eyes of those who sought to misuse them. But they were never destroyed. They endure, in fractured form, like the city itself. Like the bloodline that once ruled here."

Ryle's mind clicked into place. He had read about the Shields in the ancient texts, heard the stories of their power. But this was different. This man—this figure—spoke as if he were one of the original protectors of Omnagar, someone who had witnessed its rise and fall.

"The Master of the Shields," Ryle said, his voice catching. "Varek. He was the one who wielded them."

The figure nodded, his face still hidden beneath the dark hood. "Varek was once the greatest of us all. A scholar, a protector, a leader. He was chosen by the Shields themselves to bear their weight. But power, unchecked, corrupts. And when Varek fell, when he betrayed everything he swore to protect, the Shields—he was cast out. His legacy became one of destruction."

"But... I'm not like him," Ryle said, the words escaping his lips before he could stop them. "I don't want to be like him."

The figure's gaze, though hidden, seemed to pierce through Ryle. "You are not Varek, no. But you share his blood. And that blood calls to the Shields. You are connected to this city, to its power. You are the last of his line, the only one who can restore what was broken."

Ryle shook his head, trying to make sense of it all. "I don't understand. How can I fix this? I'm just... me. I'm not some chosen one."

"You don't have to understand," the figure said, his tone growing colder, more ominous. "The Shield has chosen you.

You have no choice. The city calls for its return. And the Black Legion—they want to use you. They want to force you to awaken the power within the Shields, to bring about a new reign of darkness."

Sarah stepped forward, her voice strong. "Then why not help us? Why not stop them?"

The figure looked at her, his eyes glowing beneath his hood. "I am not here to help. I am here to ensure the balance is restored."

The air grew tense, heavy with an energy that seemed to vibrate in the very air around them. It felt like the city itself was holding its breath, waiting for something to happen. Ryle felt a sudden surge of power, a connection between him and the city—like a thread that had been stretched thin for centuries, now snapping back into place.

"You said the Shields are connected to the city," Ryle said, his voice clearer now. "What does that mean? Why do I feel... this?" He held up the Shield, its light flickering with power.

"The Shields were created to protect Omnagar, to keep the forces of chaos from destroying everything. But when Varek betrayed them, he fractured the Shields, scattered them across the world. The city's power lies in the Shields' unity, and its fall was the result of their fragmentation. If the Shields are brought together again, the city will rise again. The balance will return."

Ryle's heart hammered in his chest. He had always known there was more to this than just the Shield he held in his hand. Omnagar, the legend of the Shields, the Black Legion—they were all tied together in a web of fate that had been spun long before he was born.

"But the Black Legion," Ryle began, his mind racing. "They want the Shields to return. They want power."

"Yes," the figure said, his voice quiet but unwavering. "The Black Legion is no longer the organization it once was. It has become an army of conquest, seeking to control the power of the Shields. And they will stop at nothing to claim what they believe is theirs."

"So how do we stop them?" Ryle asked, his voice hardening with determination. "How do we make sure they don't use the Shields to destroy the world?"

The figure's gaze darkened. "You can't. Not alone. You must find the other pieces of the Shields. Bring them together before the Legion does. And when that moment comes, you will face the Master of the Shields."

Ryle's chest tightened. The Master. Varek. The man whose name had haunted him since the moment he had first touched the Shield.

"Where do I start?" Ryle asked, his voice steady.

The figure raised his hand, pointing toward the distant horizon, toward the ruins of Omnagar.

"Where it all began," he said. "In the heart of the city. The Master's throne still stands. And the Shields... the final Shield lies there, waiting for its true bearer."

Ryle's eyes met Sarah's. They had come this far. Now, there was no turning back

# XII

# The Final Clash

The ruins of Omnagar stretched before Ryle like a labyrinth of memories, crumbling stone pillars that once held the city aloft now lying broken on the earth, suffocated by time. The wind whispered through the gaping walls, a haunting chorus of a city that had known greatness, only to fall into shadow. Yet Ryle could feel it—feel the pulsing energy beneath the ruins, the remnants of a power that still clung to the ancient stones, to the very soil.

And he knew that this was where it all ended. Or began.

His hand rested on the Shield, the warmth of it growing stronger the closer they got to the heart of Omnagar. It was calling to him, guiding him. It felt like the stone was alive, resonating with something deep inside of him. The piece of the Shield he carried was but a fraction of the whole, and as he moved deeper into the ruins, the more the connection between them seemed to grow. He could almost hear the whispers, voices of those who had come before him—the ancestors who had fought to protect Omnagar, who had been betrayed by the very power they had sworn to defend.

Ryle didn't know if it was the power of the Shield, or the weight of destiny itself, but he felt the city's memory surging through him. It felt like the air itself was charged with something ancient, a current he could not see but could feel with every breath he took.

"You feel it, don't you?" Sarah's voice broke through his thoughts, low and filled with awe.

He turned to find her standing beside him, her gaze fixed on the distant, looming structure that stood in the heart of the ruined city—the remnants of the Throne of Omnagar. It was a jagged spire of black stone, twisted and gnarled, like a crown of thorns, and it had been the seat of power for the rulers of this once-great kingdom.

"It's more than just the Shield," Ryle said, his voice carrying the weight of a thousand thoughts. "This place... it's like the city is still breathing. Still waiting for something to change."

Sarah nodded, her brow furrowed. "Waiting for you, Ryle. You're the one who's connected to it all. To the Shields. To Varek's legacy."

The name sent a shiver down his spine. Varek. The Master of the Shields. The man whose blood he shared, whose betrayal had shattered this kingdom. The man who had been the first to wield the power of the Shields, and the man who had plunged Omnagar into chaos.

Ryle clenched his fists around the Shield, the cold metal biting into his skin. "I'm not him," he muttered. "I won't be."

"You don't have a choice," Sarah said softly. "You're the last of his bloodline. That makes you the heir to the power of the Shields."

Ryle didn't respond immediately. He didn't want to think about that—the weight of it, the responsibility it carried. But he couldn't deny the truth. The city, the Shields, the legacy—it was all connected to him. To his blood. And that connection was becoming stronger, clearer with every passing moment.

"Let's get this over with," he said, his voice steady despite the storm brewing inside of him.

Together, they moved toward the Throne of Omnagar. The air grew heavier the closer they got, the temperature dropping as if the city itself was holding its breath. They reached the base of the spire, the walls slick with the remnants of age-old magic. In the center of the structure, a stone platform rose, surrounded by ancient carvings, worn and faded by centuries of time. And at the very heart of the platform, embedded in the stone, was a pedestal—the final resting place for the Shield.

Ryle stepped forward, his hand reaching for the pedestal, and as soon as his fingers brushed the stone, the world around him seemed to shift.

The Shield in his hand began to hum, its energy pulsing with an urgency that made his chest tighten. He felt something—a force—coursing through him, connecting him to the Shield, to the city, to everything that had come before him.

Then, the voice came.

It was not a voice he could hear with his ears, but a voice that resonated within him, deep and ancient.

You have come. The last of the bloodline. The true bearer of the Shields.

Ryle's heart stopped. It was as if the city itself had spoken to him.

Do you understand what you are about to awaken?

"I'm ready," Ryle whispered, though part of him trembled at the thought. He wasn't ready. But there was no choice. Not anymore.

The Shield in his hand began to glow, its light swirling around him like a storm of pure energy. The ground beneath him trembled, and suddenly, the platform split open, revealing a hidden chamber beneath the stone.

Ryle stepped forward, his heart racing. Sarah followed closely behind, her eyes wide with awe and fear.

The chamber below was vast, impossibly so. The air was thick with ancient power, and as Ryle descended into the depths, he could feel the weight of history pressing down on him. The walls of the chamber were lined with statues—guardians, protectors, their faces long faded but still full of strength. At the center of the chamber, resting on a pedestal, was the final Shield.

This one was different from the piece Ryle carried. It was whole, undamaged, and radiant with power. It pulsed with a life of its own, as if it were waiting for him, as if it recognized him as its true heir.

Ryle approached the pedestal slowly, the weight of the moment settling on his shoulders. He reached out, and as his fingers touched the Shield, the chamber shook violently, and the air crackled with energy.

The voice returned, louder now, more urgent.

The Master's blood has returned. The Shields will be whole again. But what will you choose, heir of Varek?

Ryle's breath hitched as the world around him seemed to blur. Visions of the past flooded his mind—Omnagar in its prime, the power of the Shields, the betrayal of Varek. He saw the darkness that had consumed him, the madness that had driven him to destroy everything he once loved.

Will you follow in his footsteps? Will you use the power of the Shields for conquest? For control?

Ryle's mind spun, the weight of the choice pressing on him. He knew what had to be done. The power of the Shields was too great for any one person to wield. He couldn't let history repeat itself. He couldn't let the Black Legion rise again.

"I choose to protect," Ryle said, his voice firm, though his heart was torn. "I will not be like him. I will protect what's left of this world."

The Shield in his hand flared brightly, and the room was filled with an explosion of light. For a moment, everything went dark.

When Ryle opened his eyes again, the chamber had changed. The power of the Shields had been released, but not in the way anyone had expected. It was not a weapon. It was a force of restoration, of balance. The city of Omnagar was gone, its ruins slowly crumbling, but the power of the Shields would endure.

Ryle stood there, alone for the first time in years, but not truly alone. He could feel the presence of Sarah beside him, the weight of their shared journey pulling them together. He could feel the echoes of the past and the future, the choices yet to be made.

"This isn't over, is it?" Sarah asked quietly, her eyes searching his face.

Ryle shook his head. "No. It's just beginning."

Together, they turned away from the pedestal, from the broken city of Omnagar. The Shields had been restored, but their work was not finished. The Black Legion still hunted the remnants of power, and Ryle knew that the war was far from over. The Master's shadow would not fade so easily.

But for now, Ryle had the Shield. And he had the strength to protect what remained.

The future was uncertain, but he was ready. The story of Omnagar, of the Shields, was far from over. It had only just begun.

# XIII

# The Echo and the Flame

Ashencliff smoldered in ruin.

Smoke twisted into the sky, mixing with the last light of day. The fortress of the Black Legion lay broken. Fires flickered in the shattered stone, whispering of battles past and secrets scorched by flame.

Ryle stood silently among the rubble, the last shard of the French Stone glowing faintly in his hand. Sarah ;.stood beside him, bruised but breathing, her eyes fixed on the horizon where the sea churned and wind howled like a warning.

". She's gone," Sarah whispered.

Rbbg gv f ccvf gv nh yle nodded. Verya had vanished in the final clash—swallowed by the storm, or perhaps by her own darkness. No body. No final cry. Only silence.

"We don't have all the Shields," Ryle said quietly. "Not yet."

Sarah's gaze narrowed. "And the war isn't over."

Behind them, a figure stepped from the mist—Vaelen, limping, bloodied but alive. "It never was," he said. "But you've done what few could. You chose protection over power. That matters."

He placed a hand on Ryle's shoulder. "Keep the shard safe. The rest... will come."

Ryle met his gaze. "What about Omnagar?"

Vaelen's eyes darkened. "It sleeps. But not forever."

As he turned and disappeared into the smoke, Ryle and Sarah walked away from Ashencliff's ruins, their steps slow but steady.

The wind carried the sound of old names, older wars, and a truth still unfolding.

And beneath it all, the last shard pulsed.

Not as an end.

But as a beginning.

They passed through what was left of Ashencliff's northern gate—half-shattered, blackened by fire—and entered the hollow valley beyond. The land bore scars of more than battle: it was ancient, worn by forgotten magic and broken oaths. The ground itself felt unsettled, as though disturbed by something older than memory.

Ryle clutched the shard tightly. Since the collapse, it had grown quiet. Not cold, but hushed—like it was waiting.

Sarah glanced at him. "What did it show you? Back in the tower."

He hesitated. "A city beneath Omnagar. Buried. Alive."

She didn't speak for a moment. "You think it's real?"

"I know it is," Ryle said. "And I think... I'm supposed to find it."

She nodded slowly. "Then we will."

They made camp near a stream, away from the ruins. Stars began to pierce through the smoke overhead, though some pulsed faintly, unnaturally—as if watching. Ryle sat beside the fire, the shard resting between them like a heart ripped from time.

"There were five Shields," he said. "But the Master... he had only one."

Sarah leaned forward. "Then who has the rest?"

Ryle looked into the flames. "That's what we have to find out."

In the silence that followed, a breeze stirred the grass. Faintly, on the edge of hearing, a voice echoed—not malevolent, not friendly. Just ancient.

"One falls. Another awakens."

Sarah looked around sharply. "Did you hear—?"

"I did."

They didn't sleep that night, and as dawn broke over the blackened cliffs, they turned south—toward the old paths, toward Omnagar.

Toward the truth.

The tale of the Shields was not finished. And neither were they.

Chapter 13 (continued): The Echo and the Flame

The journey south from Ashencliff was quiet.

Too quiet.

What little wildlife remained fled from the ruined coastline, and even the winds seemed to whisper warnings. Ryle, Sarah, and Vaelen—who had rejoined them at the outskirts—kept their voices low. Something about the air itself felt thin, as though the very world was holding its breath.

As they passed into the marshlands of Delmire Vale, the terrain changed: gnarled trees with bark like scorched bone leaned overhead, and moss coated the ground like silent ash. The glow of the French Stone shard pulsed faintly in

Ryle's satchel, sometimes brighter near stone relics half-sunken in the mire.

"Do you feel it?" Vaelen asked.

Sarah nodded. "Old power."

"Older than the Legion," Ryle added. "Older than even Omnagar, maybe."

They paused near a circular ruin—a dais made of white stone, cracked but not overtaken by nature. At its center, five symbols had been etched, now weathered and barely visible.

Ryle crouched and traced them with his fingers. Fire. Water. Air. Earth. Aether.

The elements of the Shields.

"These were drawn in alignment," he whispered. "This place was a gathering site. A meeting ground."

"For what?" Sarah asked, kneeling beside him.

Vaelen's eyes narrowed. "Not all the Guardians fought. Some... deliberated. There are legends of a council of wielders, one from each element. Before the Fracture."

"Before the French Stone shattered," Ryle said. "Before the world forgot."

They camped there that night, unable to push further until the mist lifted.

While Sarah slept, Ryle took the shard and sat at the center of the stone circle. As he held it in both hands, something shifted.

The air thickened.

The trees fell into silence.

Then—images.

Not visions exactly, but echoes.

A mountain bathed in lightning. A hooded figure standing in a sea of stars. A child cradling a Shield, eyes wide with fear. And finally—a city beneath the ground, its towers glass and steel, thrumming with trapped power.

Omnagar.

But... broken.

He gasped and the images shattered.

When he opened his eyes, Vaelen was standing over him.

"What did you see?"

"Fragments. Memories. I think the Shields are pulling at time. Connecting the past and future through us."

Vaelen nodded solemnly. "The power you carry, Ryle, it's more than protection or destruction. It's memory. The Shields are witnesses. They remember what the world has forgotten."

Ryle stood. "Then we need to listen."

At dawn, the trio pushed further into the Vale.

They encountered no enemies, but Ryle noticed movement—shadows in the trees, flickers of red eyes in the mist. The Black Legion hadn't been destroyed, only scattered. Somewhere out there, Verya remained.

Watching.

Waiting.

And she wasn't alone.

They reached the ruins of an old outpost by noon. Beneath its foundation was a sealed stairwell, engraved with the same five elemental marks.

Sarah brushed dust from the stone. "You think this leads to Omnagar?"

"Maybe not directly," Ryle said, "but it's a path. And I think we're supposed to take it."

He placed the shard against the center of the markings. The stone flared. The stairwell rumbled.

And slowly, it opened.

Darkness loomed below. But it was not the hollow kind. This was a darkness alive with energy—calling them downward.

Vaelen smiled grimly. "We're past the point of no return."

They descended.

One step. Then another.

And behind them, the stairway sealed.

Above, the world exhaled. Below, something ancient stirred.

Omnagar was waking.

And Ryle, Sarah, and Vaelen—shieldbearers, seekers, and survivors—would be the first to enter its depths in centuries.

The fire had been lit.

The echo carried on.

# Coming soon

Coming Soon: Volume II – The Depths of Omnagar

Beneath stone and silence, the city breathes again.

Entombed for centuries, the ruins of Omnagar awaken as Ryle, Sarah, and Vaelen journey into its forgotten heart—where the truth behind the elemental Shields lies waiting. But not all echoes of the past are dormant. As the Black Legion regathers under new command and a once-trusted friend sharpens the dagger of betrayal, the trio must navigate a maze of ancient technology, buried secrets, and the unsettling realization that the Fracture was only the beginning. Loyalties will falter. Powers will evolve. And in the lightless corridors of the old world, something older than war watches with patient eyes.

Omnagar has opened. And it remembers everything.